It was still snowing.

It was Lisa's childhood dream of a white Christmas come true. And to think that if she had returned to London as she had originally planned to do, she would have missed it! Emotion caught her by the throat.

"It's so magical. This house...the weather... the tree...church this morning...my stocking and..."

"And...?" Oliver prompted softly.

He was looking at her very intently—so intently, in fact, that she felt as though she could drown in his eyes.

"And you," she breathed, and as she said it she felt her heart slam fiercely against her chest wall, depriving her of breath while the silence between them seemed to pulse and quicken and take on a life of its own.

PENNY JORDAN was constantly in trouble in school because of her inability to stop daydreaming—especially during French lessons. In her teens, she was an avid romance reader, although it didn't occur to her to try writing one herself until she was older. "My first half-dozen attempts ended up ingloriously," she remembers, "but I persevered, and one manuscript was finished." She plucked up the courage to send it to a publisher, convinced her book would be rejected. It wasn't, and the rest is history! Penny is married and lives in Cheshire, England.

Penny Jordan's striking mainstream novel *Power Play* quickly became a *New York Times* bestseller. She followed that success with *Silver*, *The Hidden Years*, *Lingering Shadows*, *For Better For Worse*, *Cruel Legacy* and, her latest, *Power Games*.

"Women everywhere will find pieces of themselves in Jordan's characters."

—*Publishers Weekly* on *For Better For Worse*

Books by Penny Jordan

PENNY JORDAN

Her Christmas Fantasy

Harlequin Books

TORONTO • NEW YORK • LONDON
AMSTERDAM • PARIS • SYDNEY • HAMBURG
STOCKHOLM • ATHENS • TOKYO • MILAN
MADRID • WARSAW • BUDAPEST • AUCKLAND

ISBN 0-373-11851-1

HER CHRISTMAS FANTASY

First North American Publication 1996.

Copyright © 1996 by Penny Jordan.

This edition published by arrangement with Harlequin Books S.A.

® and TM are trademarks of the publisher. Trademarks indicated with ® are registered in the United States Patent and Trademark Office, the Canadian Trade Marks Office and in other countries.

Printed in U.S.A.

CHAPTER ONE

LISA paused hesitantly outside the shop, studying the very obviously designer-label and expensive outfits in the window doubtfully.

She had been given the address by a friend who had told her that the shop was one of the most exclusive 'nearly new' designer-clothes outlets in the city, where outfits could be picked up for less than a third of their original price.

Lisa was no fashion victim—normally she was quite happy with her small wardrobe of good-quality chain-store clothes—but Henry had seemed so anxious that she create a good impression on his family and their friends, and most particularly his mother, during their Christmas visit to his parents' home in the north that Lisa had felt obliged to take the hints he had been dropping and add something rather more up-market to her wardrobe. Especially since Henry had already indicated that he wanted to put their relationship on a more formal basis, with an official announcement to his family of their plans to marry.

Lisa knew that many of her friends found Henry slightly stuffy and old-fashioned, but she liked those aspects of his personality. They indicated a reliability, a dependability in him which, so far as she was concerned, outweighed his admitted tendency to fuss and find fault over minor details.

When the more outspoken of her closest friends had asked her what she saw in him she'd told them quietly that she saw a dependable husband and a good father.

'But what about romance?' they had asked her. 'What about falling desperately and passionately in love?'

Lisa had laughed, genuinely amused.

'I'm not the type of woman who falls desperately or passionately in love,' she had responded, 'and nor do I want to be!'

'But doesn't it annoy you that Henry's so chauvinistically old-fashioned?' Her friends had persisted. 'Look at the way he's fussing over you meeting his parents and family—telling you how he wants you to dress.'

'He's just anxious for me to make a good impression,' Lisa had argued back on Henry's behalf. 'He obviously values his parents' opinion and—'

'And he's still tied to his mother's apron strings,' one of her friends had scoffed. 'I know the type.' She had paused a little before adding more seriously, 'You know, don't you, that he was on the point of becoming engaged to someone else shortly before he met you and that he broke off the relationship because he wasn't sure that his family would approve of her? Apparently they're very old-fashioned and strait-laced, and Janey had been living with someone else when she'd first met Henry—'

'Yes, I do know,' Lisa had retorted firmly. 'But the reason that they broke up was not Janey's past history but that Henry realised that they didn't, simply *didn't* have enough in common.'

'And you and he do?' her friend had asked drily.

'We both want the same things out of life, yes,' Lisa had asserted defensively.

And it was, after all, true. She might not have fallen deeply in love with Henry the night they were introduced by a mutual friend, but she had certainly liked him enough to accept his invitation to dinner, and their relationship had grown steadily from that date to the point where they both felt that their future lay together.

She might not be entirely comfortable with Henry's insistence that she buy herself a new wardrobe in order to impress his wealthy parents and their circle of friends, but she could sympathise with the emotion which had led to him making such a suggestion.

Her own parents would, she knew, be slightly bemused by her choice of a husband; her mother was a gifted and acclaimed potter whose work was internationally praised, whilst her father's stylish, modern furniture designs meant that he was constantly in demand, not just as a designer but as a lecturer as well.

Both her parents were currently in Japan, and were not due to return for another two months.

It would have been a lonely Christmas for her this year if Henry had not invited her to go north with him to the Yorkshire Dales to visit his parents, Lisa acknowledged.

He had already warned her that his parents might consider her work as a PA to the owner of a small, London-based antique business rather too bohemian and arty. Had she worked in industry, been a teacher or a nurse, they would have found it more acceptable.

'In fact they'd probably prefer it if you didn't work at all,' he had told Lisa carefully when they had been discussing the subject.

'Not work? But that's—' Hastily she had bitten back the words she had been about to say, responding mildly instead, 'Most women these days expect to have a career.'

'My mother doesn't approve of married women working, especially when they have children,' Henry had told her stiffly.

Firmly suppressing her instinctive response that his mother was very obviously rather out of touch with modern life, Lisa had said placatingly instead, 'A lot of women tend to put their career on hold or work part-time when their children are young.'

She had hesitated outside the shop for long enough, she decided now, pushing open the door and walking in.

The young girl who came forward to help her explained that she was actually standing in for the owner of the shop, who had been called away unexpectedly.

The clothes on offer were unexpectedly wearable, Lisa acknowledged, and not too over-the-top as she had half dreaded. One outfit in particular caught her eye—a trouser suit in fine cream wool crêpe which comprised trousers, waistcoat and jacket.

'It's an Armani,' the salesgirl enthused as Lisa picked it off the rail. 'A real bargain... I was tempted to buy it myself,' she admitted, 'but it's only a size ten and I take a twelve. It's this season's stock—a real bargain.'

'This season's.' A small frown puckered Lisa's forehead. Who on earth these days could afford to buy a designer outfit and then get rid of it within a few months of buying it—especially something like this in such a classical design that it wasn't going to date?

'If you like it, we've got several other things in from the same per... the same source,' the girl was telling her. 'Would you like to see them?'

Lisa paused and then smiled her agreement. She was beginning to enjoy this rather more than she had expected. The feel of the cream crêpe beneath her fingertips was sensuously luxurious. She had always loved fabrics, their textures, differing weights.

An hour later, her normally immaculate long bob of silky blonde hair slightly tousled from all her trying on, she grimaced ruefully at the pile of clothes that she had put to one side as impossible to resist.

What woman, having bought such a luxuriously expensive and elegantly wearable wardrobe, could bear to part with it after so short a period of time?

If she had been given free rein to choose from new herself, she could not have chosen better, Lisa recognised as she sighingly acknowledged that the buttermilk-coloured silk, wool and cashmere coat she had just tried on was an absolute must.

She was, she admitted ten minutes later as she took a deep breath and signed her credit-card bill, buying these clothes not so much for Henry and his family as for herself.

'You've got an absolute bargain,' the salesgirl told her unnecessarily as she carefully wrapped Lisa's purchases in tissue-paper and put them into several large, glossy carrier bags.

'I think these are the nicest things we've had in in a long time. Personally I don't think I could have brought myself to part with them ... That coat...' She gave a small sigh and then told Lisa half enviously, 'They fitted you perfectly as well. I envy you being so tall and slim.'

'So tall.' Lisa winced slightly. She wasn't excessively tall, being five feet nine, but she was aware that with Henry being a rather stocky five feet ten or so he preferred her not to wear high-heeled shoes, and he had on occasion made rather irritated comments to her about her height.

She was just on her way out of the shop when a car drew up outside, its owner double parking in flagrant disregard for the law.

He looked extremely irritable and ill-tempered, Lisa decided as she watched him stride towards the shop, and wondered idly who he was.

Not a prospective customer, even on behalf of a woman friend. No, he was quite definitely the type who, if he did buy clothes for a woman, would not need to exercise financial restraint by buying them second-hand.

Lisa was aware of his frown deepening as he glanced almost dismissively at her.

Well, she was equally unimpressed by him, she decided critically. Stunningly, almost overpoweringly male he might look, with that tall, broad-shouldered body and that hawkish, arrogant profile, but he was simply not her type.

She had no doubt that the more romantic of her friends would consider him ideal 'swoon over' material, with those frowning, overtly sexual, strongly drawn male features and his dominant masterful manner. But she merely thought him arrogantly over-confident. Look at the way he had dismissed her with the briefest of irritable glances, stalking past her. Even the silky gleam of his thick dark hair possessed a strong air of male sexuality.

He would be the kind of man who looked almost too hirsute with his clothes off, she decided unkindly, sternly suppressing the impish little demon of rebellion within her that immediately produced a very clear and highly erotic mental image of him thus unclad and, to her exasperation, not overly hirsute at all... In fact...

Stop it, she warned herself as she flagged down a cruising taxi and gave the driver the address of the friend who had recommended the shop to her.

She had promised her that she would call round and let her know how she had fared, but for some reason, once her purchases had been duly displayed and enviously approved, she discovered that Alison was more interested in hearing about the man she had passed in the street than discussing the likelihood of her forthcoming introduction to Henry's parents' going well.

'He wasn't my type at all,' she declared firmly to Alison. 'He was far too arrogant. I don't imagine he would have the first idea of how to treat a modern woman—'

'You mean that Henry does...?' Alison asked drily, stopping Lisa in her tracks for a moment before she valiantly responded.

'Of course he does.'

'You just wait,' Alison warned her. 'The moment he gets that ring on your finger, he's going to start nagging you to conform. He'll want you to stop working, for a start. Look at the way he goes on about what a perfect mother his own mother was...how she devoted her life to his father and himself...'

'I think it's rather touching that he's so devoted to her, so loyal and loving...' Lisa defended.

'Mmm... What's he like in bed?' Alison asked her curiously.

Even though Lisa was used to her friend's forthrightness, she was a little taken aback by her question, caught too off guard to do anything other than answer honestly.

'I...I don't know... We...we haven't... We don't...'

'You don't *know*. Are you crazy? You're planning to *marry* the man and you don't know yet what he's like in bed. How long have you two known one another?'

'Almost eight months,' Lisa replied slightly stiffly.

'Mmm... Hardly the type to be overwhelmed by passion, then, is he, our Henry?'

'Henry believes in old-fashioned courtship, that couples should get to know one another as...as people. He doesn't...he doesn't care for the modern approach to casual sex...'

'Very laudable,' Alison told her sardonically.

'Look, the fact that we haven't...that we don't...that we haven't been to bed together yet isn't a problem for *me*,' Lisa told her vehemently.

'No? Then it should be,' Alison returned forthrightly. 'How on earth can you think of marrying a man when you don't even know if the two of you are sexually compatible yet?'

'Easily,' Lisa replied promptly. 'After all, our grandparents did.'

Alison rolled her eyes and mocked, 'And you claim that you aren't romantic.'

'It takes more to build a good marriage than just sex,' Lisa told her quietly. 'I'm tired of men who take you out for dinner and then expect you to take them to bed as a thank-you... I want stability in a relationship, Alison. Someone I can rely on, depend on. Someone who respects and values me as a *person*... Yes, all right, Henry might be slightly old-fashioned and...and...'

'Sexless?' her friend came back, but Lisa shook her head and continued determinedly.

'But he's very loyal...very faithful...very trustworthy...and...'

'If that's what you're looking for you'd be better off with a dog,' Alison suggested critically, but Lisa wasn't prepared to argue the matter any further.

'I'm just not the type for excitement and passion,' she told her friend. 'I like stability. Marriage isn't just for now, Alison; it's for the future too. Look, I'd better go,' she announced, glancing at her watch. 'Henry's taking me out for dinner this evening.' As she got up and headed for the door, she added gratefully, 'Thanks for recommending that shop to me.'

'Yes, I'm really envious. You've got some lovely things and at a knock-down price. All current season's stuff too... Lucky you.'

*   *   *

As she made her way home to her own flat Lisa was ruefully aware of how difficult her friends found it to understand her relationship with Henry, but then they had not had her upbringing and did not possess her desire—her craving in a sense—for emotional tranquillity, for roots and permanence.

Her parents were both by nature not just extremely artistic—and because of that at times wholly absorbed by their work—they were also gypsies, nomads, who enjoyed travelling and moving on. The thought of basing themselves somewhere permanently was anathema to them.

During her childhood Lisa couldn't remember having spent a whole year at any one school; she knew her parents loved her, and she certainly loved them dearly, but she had a different nature from theirs.

All right, so she knew that it would be difficult persuading Henry to accept that there was no reason why she should not still pursue her career as well as being a mother, but she was sure that she would be able to make him understand that her work was important to her. At the moment Henry worked for a prestigious firm of insurance brokers, but they had both agreed that once they were married they would move out of London and into the country.

She let herself into her small flat and carefully carried her new purchases into her bedroom.

After she had had a shower she intended to try them all on again, if she had time before Henry arrived. However, when she replayed her answering-machine tape there was a message on it from Henry, cancelling their date because he had an important business dinner that he had to attend and reminding her that they still had to shop for suitable Christmas presents to take for his family.

She had already made several suggestions based on what Henry had told her about his family, and specifically his parents—a very pretty petit point antique footstool for his grandmother, some elegant tulip vases for his mother, who, he had told her, was a keen gardener. But Henry had pursed his lips and dismissed her ideas.

She had been tempted to suggest that it might be better if he chose their Christmas presents on his own, but she had warned herself that she was being unfair and even slightly petty. He, after all, knew their tastes far better than she did.

She had just put on her favourite of all the outfits she had bought—the cream wool crêpe trouser suit—when her doorbell rang.

Assuming that it must be Henry after all, she went automatically to open the door, and then stood staring in total shock as she realised that her visitor wasn't Henry but the man she had last seen striding past her and storming into the dress agency as she'd left it.

'Lisa Phillips?' he demanded curtly as he stepped past her and into her hall.

Dumbly Lisa nodded her head, too taken aback by the unexpectedness of his arrival to think to question his right to walk uninvited into her home.

'My name's Oliver Davenport,' he told her curtly, handing her a card, barely giving her time to glance at it before he continued, 'I believe you purchased several items of clothing from Second Time Around earlier today.'

'Er...yes,' Lisa agreed. 'But—'

'Good. This shouldn't take long then. Unfortunately the clothes that you bought should not have been put on sale. Technically, in fact, the shop sold them without the permission of their true owner, and in such circumstances, as with the innocent purchase of a stolen

car or indeed any stolen goods, you have no legal right
to—'

'Just a minute,' she interrupted him in disbelief.
Completely taken aback by his unexpected arrival and
his infuriatingly arrogant manner, Lisa could feel herself
becoming thoroughly angry. 'Are you accusing the shop
of selling stolen clothes? Because if so it should be the
police you are informing and not me.'

'Not exactly. Look, I'm prepared to refund you the
full amount of what you spent plus an extra hundred
pounds for any inconvenience. So if you'll just—'

'That's very generous of you,' Lisa told him sarcastically. 'But I bought these clothes for a specific purpose
and I have no intention of selling them back to you. I
bought them in good faith and—'

'Look, I've just explained to you, those clothes should
never have been sold in the first place,' he cut across her
harshly, giving her an impatiently angry look.

Lisa didn't like the way he was filling her small hall,
looming almost menacingly over her, but there was no
way she was going to give in to him. Why should she?

'If that's true, then why hasn't the shop been in touch
with me?' Lisa challenged him.

She could see that he didn't like her question from
the way his mouth tightened and hardened before he replied bitingly, 'Probably because the idiotic woman who
runs the place refuses to listen to reason.'

'Really?' Lisa asked him scathingly. 'You seem to have
a way with women. Has it ever occurred to you that a
little less aggression and a good deal more persuasion
might produce better results? Not that any amount of
persuasion will change my mind,' she added firmly. 'I
bought those clothes in good faith, and since the shop
hasn't seen fit to get in touch with me concerning their
supposedly wrongful sale I don't see why—'

'Oh, for God's sake.' She was interrupted furiously. 'Look, if you must know, the clothes belong to my cousin's girlfriend. They had a quarrel—it's a very volatile relationship. She walked out on him, vowing never to come back—they'd had an argument about her decision to go on holiday with a girlfriend, without him apparently—and in a fit of retaliatory anger he gave her clothes to the dress agency. It was an impulse . . . something he regretted virtually as soon as he'd done it, and when Emma rang him from Italy to make things up he asked me to help him get her things back before she comes home and discovers what he's done.'

'He asked *you* for help?'

There was very little doubt in Lisa's mind about whose girlfriend the absent Emma actually was, and it wasn't Oliver Davenport's fictitious cousin.

The look he gave her in response to her question wasn't very friendly, Lisa recognised; in fact it wasn't very friendly at all, but even though, concealed beneath the sensual elegance of her newly acquired trousers, her knees were knocking slightly, she refused to give in to her natural apprehension.

It wasn't like her to be so stubborn or so unsympathetic, but something about him just seemed to rub her up the wrong way and make her uncharacteristically antagonistic towards him.

It wasn't just the fact that he was demanding that she part with her newly acquired wardrobe that was making her combative, she admitted; it was something about the man himself, something about his arrogance, his . . . his maleness that was setting her nerves slightly on edge, challenging her into a mode of behaviour that was really quite foreign to her.

She knew that Henry would have been shocked to see her displaying so much stubbornness and anger—she was a little bit shocked herself.

'He was about to go away on business. Emma's due back at the end of the week. He didn't want her walking into the flat and discovering that half her clothes are missing...'

'No, I'm sure you...he...' Lisa corrected herself tauntingly '...doesn't...'

She saw from the dark burn of angry colour etching his cheekbones that he wasn't pleased by her deliberate 'mistake', nor the tone of voice she had delivered it in.

'You have no legal claim over those clothes,' he told her grimly. 'The shop sold them without the owner's permission.'

'If that's true, then it's up to the shop to get in touch with me,' Lisa pointed out. 'After all, for all I know, you could want them for yourself...' She paused. His temper was set on a hair-trigger already and although she doubted that he would actually physically harm her...

'Don't be ridiculous,' she heard him breathe softly, as though he had read her mind.

Inexplicably she realised that she was blushing slightly as, for no logical reason at all, she remembered exactly what she had been thinking about him—and his body— earlier in the day. Just as well he hadn't second guessed her private thoughts *then*!

'So you're not prepared to be reasonable about this?'

She be reasonable? Lisa could feel her own temper starting to rise.

'Doesn't it mean anything to you that you could be putting someone's whole relationship at risk by your refusal?'

'*Me* putting a relationship at risk?' Lisa gasped at the unfairness of it. 'If you ask me, I'm not the one who's doing that. If your relationship is so important to you you should have thought of that before you lost your temper and decided to punish your girlfriend by selling her clothes—'

'Emma is not *my* girlfriend,' he told her with ominous calm. 'As I've already explained to you, I am simply acting as an intermediary in all of this for my cousin. But then I suppose it's par for the course that you should think otherwise. It goes with all the rest of your illogical behaviour,' he told her scathingly.

'If you ask me,' she told him, thoroughly incensed now, 'I think that Emma...whoever's girlfriend she is— yours or your cousin's...is better off without you. What kind of man does something like that...? Those clothes were virtually new and—'

'Exactly. New and expensive and paid for by my cousin, who is a rather jealous young man who objects to his girlfriend wearing the clothes he bought her to attract the attentions of other men...'

'And because of that he stole them from her wardrobe and sold them? It sounds to me as though she's better off without you...without him,' Lisa corrected herself fiercely, her eyes showing her contempt of a man—any man—jealous or otherwise, who could behave in such a petty and revengeful way.

'Well, I'm sorry,' she continued, patently anything but. 'But explaining to Emma just exactly what's happened to her clothes is your problem and not mine. I bought them in good faith—'

'And you'll be able to buy some more with the money I'm willing to refund you for them, especially since... Oh, I get it,' he said softly, his eyes suddenly narrowing.

'You get what?' Lisa demanded suspiciously, not liking the cynicism she could see in his eyes. 'Those clothes were virtually brand-new, this season's stock, and I'd be very lucky indeed to pick up anything else like them at such a bargain price, especially at this time of year, and—'

'Oh, yes, I can see what you're after. All right then, I don't like blackmailers and I wouldn't normally give in to someone who plainly thinks she's onto a good thing, but I haven't got time to waste negotiating with you. What would you guess was the full, brand-new value of the clothes you bought today?'

'The full value?' A small frown puckered Lisa's forehead. She had no idea at all of what he was getting at. 'I have no idea. I don't normally buy exclusive designer-label clothes, especially not Armani...but I imagine it would have to be several thousand pounds...'

'Several thousand pounds.' A thin, dangerous smile curled his mouth, his eyes so coldly contemptuous that Lisa actually felt a small, icy shiver race down her spine.

'Why don't we settle for a round figure and make it five thousand pounds? I'll write you a cheque for five thousand here and now and you'll give me back Emma's clothes.'

Lisa stared at him in disbelief.

'But that's crazy,' she protested. 'Why on earth should you pay me five thousand pounds when you could go out and buy a whole new wardrobe for her for that amount...?' She shook her head in disbelief. 'I don't—'

'Oh, come on,' he interrupted her cuttingly. 'Don't give me that. You understand perfectly well. Even *I* understand how impossible and time-wasting an exercise it would be for me to go out and replace every single item with its exact replica...even if I knew what it was I was supposed to be buying. Don't overplay your hand,' he warned her. 'All that mock innocence doesn't suit you.'

Mock innocence!

As she suddenly recognised just what he was accusing her of, Lisa's face flushed a brilliant, furious scarlet.

'Get out... Get out of my flat right now,' she demanded shakily. 'Otherwise I'm going to call the police. How dare you accuse me of...of...?' She couldn't even say the word, she felt such a sense of outrage and disgust.

'I wouldn't give you those clothes now if you offered to pay me ten thousand...twenty thousand,' she told him passionately. 'You deserve to lose Emma... In fact, I think I'm probably doing her a favour by letting her see just what kind of a man you are. I suppose you thought that just because you bought her clothes for her you had a right to...to take them back... If I were her... If I were her...'

'Yes? If you were her, what?' he goaded her, just as furious as she was herself, Lisa recognised as she saw the small pulse beating fiercely in his jaw and the banked-down fury in his eyes.

'I wouldn't have let you buy them for me in the first place,' she threw emotionally at him, adding, 'I'd rather—'

'Rather what?' he challenged her, his voice dropping suddenly and becoming dangerously, sensually soft as he raked her from head to foot in such a sexually predatory and searching way that it left her virtually shaking, trembling, her body overreacting wildly to the male sexuality in the way he was looking at her, the sensual challenge in the way his eyes deliberately stripped her of her clothes, leaving her body vulnerable... exposed...naked.

'You'd rather what?' he repeated triumphantly. 'Go naked?'

Lisa couldn't speak; she was too shocked, too outraged, too aware of her feminine vulnerability to the blazing heat of his sexuality to risk saying anything.

'But then in actual fact, according to you—since you refuse to believe the truth and accept that I am acting for my cousin and not for myself—you are wearing clothes that I have chosen...bought...' he added softly, his glance slipping suggestively over her body for a second time, but this time more slowly, more lingeringly...more...more seductively, Lisa recognised as she felt herself responding helplessly to the sheer force of the magnetic spell he seemed to have cast over her.

From somewhere she managed to find the strength to break free. Stepping back from him, putting a safer distance between them, averting her eyes and her overflushed face from his powerful gaze, she demanded huskily, 'I want you to leave. Now. Otherwise...'

'You'll call the police. I know,' he agreed drily. 'Very well, since it's obvious I can't make you see reason... I won't forget how co-operative you've been,' he added, sending a small shiver down her spine as she saw the look in his eyes. 'Although I can understand why you're so loath to part with your borrowed finery.

'The suit looks good on you,' he added unexpectedly as he turned towards the door, pausing to look at her before lifting his hand and outrageously tracing a line with the tip of his index finger all the way along the deep V of the neckline of the waistcoat just where the upper curves of her breasts, naked underneath it, pressed against the creamy fabric.

'It's a bit tighter here on you than it was on Emma, though,' he told her. 'She's probably only a 34B whereas you must be a 34C. Nice—especially worn the way you're wearing it now, without anything underneath it...'

Lisa swallowed back all of the agitated, defensive remarks that sprang to her lips, knowing that none of them could do anything to wipe out what he had just said to her, or the effect his words had had on her.

Why, she wondered wretchedly as he opened her front door and left her flat far more calmly than he had entered it, did her body have to react so... so... idiotically and erotically to his touch? Even without looking down she knew how betrayingly her nipples were still pressing against the fine fabric of her waistcoat—as they certainly hadn't been doing when he'd first arrived. As they had, in fact, only humiliatingly done when he had reached out and touched her with that lazily mocking fingertip which had had such a devastating effect on her senses.

It was because she was so overwrought, that was all, she tried to comfort herself half an hour later, the front door securely bolted as she hugged a comforting mug of freshly made coffee.

She would have to ring the shop, of course, and find out exactly what was going on, and if they asked her to return the clothes then morally she would have no option other than to do so.

How dared he accuse her of trying to blackmail him...? *Her*. The coffee slopped out of the mug as her hands started to shake. As if she would ever... ever do any such thing. She felt desperately sorry for the unknown Emma. It was bad enough that he should have sold her clothes, but how would she feel, knowing that he had touched her, another woman, so... so...? No, in her view Emma was better off without him. Much better off.

How dared he touch her like that... as though... as though...? And he had known exactly what he was doing as well. She had seen it in those shockingly knowing steel-grey eyes as she'd read the message of male triumph and awareness that they'd been giving her. He had known that he was arousing her—had known it and had enjoyed knowing it.

Unlike her. She had hated it and she hated him. Emma was quite definitely better off without him and she certainly wasn't going to be the one to help him make up their quarrel by returning her clothes.

At least he was not likely to be able to carry out that subtle threat of future retribution against her—thank goodness.

CHAPTER TWO

LISA stood in front of the guest-bedroom window of Henry's parents' large Victorian house looking out across the wintry countryside.

They had arrived considerably later than expected the previous evening, due, in the main, to the fact that Henry's car had been so badly damaged whilst parked in a client's car park that their departure had been delayed and they had had to use her small—much smaller—model, much to Henry's disgust.

They had arrived shortly after eleven o'clock, and whilst Henry had been greeted with a good deal of maternal anxiety and concern Lisa had received a considerably more frosty reception, Henry's mother giving her a chilly smile and presenting a cool cheek for her to kiss before commenting, 'I'm afraid we couldn't put back supper any longer. You know what your father's like about meal times, Henry.'

'It was Lisa's fault,' Henry had grumbled untruthfully, adding to Lisa, 'You really should get a decent car, you know. Oh, and by the way, you need petrol.'

Lisa had gritted her teeth and smiled, reminding herself that she had already guessed from Henry's comments about his family that, as an only child and a son, he was the apple of his mother's eye.

Whilst Henry had been despatched to his father's study, Lisa had been quizzed by Henry's mother about her family and background. It had subtly been made plain to Lisa that so far as Henry's mother was concerned the jury was still out on the subject of her suitability as Henry's intended wife.

Normally she would have enjoyed the chance to visit the Yorkshire Dales, Lisa acknowledged—especially at this time of the year. Last night she had been enchanted to discover that snow was expected on the high ground.

Henry had been less impressed. In fact, he had been in an edgy, difficult mood throughout the entire journey—and not just, Lisa suspected, because of the damage to his precious car.

It had struck her, over the previous weekend, when they'd been doing the last of their Christmas shopping together, that he was obviously having doubts about her ability to make the right impression on his parents. There had been several small lectures and clumsy hints on what his family would expect, and one particularly embarrassing moment when Alison had called round to the flat just as Henry had been explaining that he wasn't sure that the Armani trouser suit was going to be quite the thing for his parents' annual pre-Christmas supper party.

'What century are Henry's parents living in?' Alison had exploded after Henry had left the room. 'Honestly, Lisa, I can't—'

She had stopped when Lisa had shaken her head, changing the subject to ask instead, 'Any more repercussions about the clothes you bought from Second Time Around, by the way?'

Lisa had told Alison all about her run-in with Oliver Davenport, asking her friend's advice as to what she ought to do.

'Ring the shop and find out what they've got to say,' had been Alison's prompt response.

'I've already done that,' Lisa had told her. 'And there was just a message on the answering machine saying that the owner has had to close the shop down indefinitely because her father has been taken seriously ill.'

'Well, if you want my opinion, you bought those clothes in all good faith, and I feel that their original owner deserves to know exactly what kind of miserable rat her boyfriend is... I mean...selling her clothes... It's...it's... Well, I'd certainly never forgive any man who tried to pull that one on me. I think you did exactly the right thing in refusing to give them back,' Alison had said comfortingly.

'No. No further repercussions,' Lisa had told her in response to her latest question. 'Which I find surprising. I suppose I did overreact a little bit, but when he virtually accused me of trying to blackmail him into paying almost more for them than they had originally cost...'

Her voice had quivered with remembered indignation as she recalled how shocked and insulted she had felt to be confronted with such a contemptuous assessment of her character.

'You overreacting—and to a man... Now that's something I *would* like to see,' Alison had told her.

'Who are you discussing?' Henry had asked, coming back into the room.

'Oh, no one special,' Lisa had told him, hastily and untruthfully, hoping that he wouldn't question the sudden surge of hot, guilty colour flooding her face as she remembered the shocking unexpectedness and intimacy of the way Oliver Davenport had reached out and touched her, and her even more shocking and intimate reaction to his touch.

The whole incident was something that was best forgotten she told herself firmly now as she craned her neck to watch a shepherd manoeuvring his flock on the distant hillside. She felt very sorry for Emma, of course, in the loss of her clothes, but hopefully it would teach Oliver

Davenport not to behave so arrogantly in future. It was certainly a lesson he needed to learn.

Lisa glanced at her watch.

Henry's mother had announced last night that they sat down for breakfast at eight o'clock sharp, the implication being that she suspected that Lisa lived too decadent and lazy a lifestyle to manage to get up early enough to join them.

She couldn't have been more wrong, Lisa acknowledged. She was normally a very early riser.

The build-up to Christmas, and most especially the week before it, was normally one of her favourite times of the year. Her parents might live a rather unconventional lifestyle by Henry's parents' standards, but wherever they had lived when she'd been a child they had always made a point of following as many Christmas traditions as they could—buying and dressing a specially chosen Christmas tree, cooking certain favourite Christmas treats, shopping for presents and wrapping them. But Lisa had always yearned for the trappings of a real British Christmas. She had been looking forward to seeing such a traditional scenario of events taking place in Henry's childhood home, but it had become apparent to her the previous evening that Henry's parents, and more specifically Henry's mother, did not view Christmas in the same way she did herself.

'The whole thing has become so dreadfully commercialised that I simply don't see the point nowadays,' she had commented when Lisa had been describing the fun she had had shopping for gifts for the several small and *not* so small children who featured on her Christmas present list.

Her father in particular delighted in receiving anything toy-like, and had a special weakness for magic tricks. Lisa had posted her gifts to her parents to Japan weeks ago, and had, in turn, received hers from them. She had brought the presents north with her, intending to add them to the pile she had assumed would accumulate beneath the Christmas tree, which in her imagination she had visualised as tall and wonderfully bushy, dominating the large hallway that Henry had described to her, warmed by the firelight of its open hearth and scenting the whole room with the delicious aroma of fresh pine needles.

Alas for her imaginings. Henry's mother did not, apparently, like real Christmas trees. They caused too much mess with their needles. And as for an open fire! They had had that boarded up years ago, she had informed Lisa, adding that it had caused far too much mess and nuisance.

So much for her hazy thoughts of establishing the beginnings of their own family traditions, her plans of one day telling her own children how she and their father had spent their first Christmas together, going out to choose the family Christmas tree.

'You're far too romantic and impractical,' Henry had criticised her. 'I agree with Mother. Real Christmas trees are nothing but a nuisance.'

As she turned away from the window Lisa was uncomfortably aware not only of Henry's mother's reluctance to accept her, but also of her own unexpectedly rebellious feeling that Henry was letting her down in not being more supportive of her.

She hadn't spent one full day with Henry's family yet, and already she was beginning to regret the extended length of their Christmas stay with them.

Reluctantly she walked towards the bedroom door. It was ten to eight, and the last thing she wanted to do now was arrive late for breakfast.

*   *   *

'Off-white wool... Don't you think that's rather impractical?' Henry's mother asked Lisa critically.

Taking a deep breath and counting to ten, Lisa forced herself to smile as she responded politely to Mary Hanford's criticism.

'Perhaps a little, but then—'

'I never wear cream or white. I think they can be so draining to the pale English complexion,' her prospective mother-in-law continued. 'Navy is always so much more serviceable, I think.'

Lisa had arrived downstairs half an hour ago, all her offers to help with the preparation of the pre-Christmas buffet supper having been firmly refused.

So much for creating the right impression on Henry's parents with her new clothes, Lisa reflected wryly, wishing that Alison was with her to appreciate the ironic humour of the situation.

She could, of course, have shared the joke with Henry, but somehow she doubted that he would have found it funny... He had, no doubt, inherited his sense of humour, or rather his lack of it, from his mother, she decided sourly, and was immediately ashamed of her own mean-spiritedness.

Of course, it was only natural that Henry's mother should be slightly distant with her. Naturally she was protective of Henry—he was her only son, her only child...

He was also a man of thirty-one, a sharp inner voice reminded Lisa, and surely capable of making his own mind up about who he wanted to marry? Or was he?

It hadn't escaped Lisa's notice during the day how Henry consistently and illuminatingly agreed with whatever opinion his mother chose to voice, but she dismissed the tiny niggling doubts that were beginning to undermine her confidence in her belief that she and

Henry had a future together as natural uncertainties raised by seeing him in an unfamiliar setting and with people, moreover, who knew him far better than she did.

In the hallway the grandfather clock chimed the hour. In a few minutes the Hanfords' supper guests would be arriving.

Henry had already explained to her that his family had lived in the area for several generations and that they had a large extended family, most of whom would be at the supper party, along with a handful of his parents' friends.

Lisa was slightly apprehensive aware that she would be very much on show, which was one of the reasons why she had chosen to wear the cream trouser suit.

Henry, however, hadn't been any more approving of her outfit than his mother, telling her severely that he thought that a skirt would have been more appropriate than trousers.

Lisa had no doubt that Oliver Davenport would have been both highly amused and contemptuous of her failure to achieve the desired effect with her acquired plumage.

Oliver Davenport. Now what on earth was she doing thinking about such a disagreeable subject, such a contentious person, when by rights she ought to be concentrating on the evening ahead of her?

'Ah, Lisa, there you are!' she heard Henry exclaiming. 'Everyone will be arriving soon, and Mother likes us all to be in the hall to welcome them when they do.

'I see you didn't change after all,' he added, frowning at her.

'An Armani suit is a perfectly acceptable outfit to wear for a supper party, Henry,' Lisa pointed out mildly, and couldn't help adding a touch more robustly, 'And, to be honest, I think I would have felt rather cold in a skirt. Your parents—'

'Mother doesn't think an overheated house is healthy,' Henry interrupted her quickly—so quickly that Lisa suspected that she wasn't the first person to comment on the chilliness of his parents' house.

'I expect I'm feeling the cold because we're so much further north here,' she offered diplomatically as she followed him into the hallway.

Cars could be heard pulling up outside, their doors opening and closing.

'That's good!' Henry exclaimed. 'Mother likes everyone to be on time.'

Mother would, Lisa thought rebelliously, but wisely she kept the words to herself.

Henry's aunt and her family were the first to arrive. A smaller, quieter edition of her elder sister, she was, nevertheless, far warmer in her manner towards Lisa than Henry's mother had been, and Lisa didn't miss the looks exchanged by her three teenage children as they were subjected to Mary Hanford's critical inspection.

Fifteen minutes later the hallway was virtually full, and Lisa was beginning to lose track of just who everyone was. The doorbell rang again and Henry went to answer it. As Lisa turned to look at the newcomers her heart suddenly stood still and then gave a single shocked bound followed by a flurry of too fast, disbelieving, nervous beats.

Oliver Davenport! What on earth was he doing here? He couldn't have followed her here to pursue his demand for her to return Emma's clothes, could he?

At the thought of what Henry's mother was likely to say if Oliver Davenport caused the same kind of scene here in public as he had staged in the privacy of her own flat, Lisa closed her eyes in helpless dismay, and then heard Henry saying tensely to her, 'Lisa, I'd like to introduce you to one of my parents' neighbours. Oliver—'

'Lisa and I already know one another.'

Lisa's eyes widened in bemused incomprehension.

Oliver Davenport was a neighbour of Henry's parents! And what did he mean by implying that they knew one another... by saying her name in that grossly deceptive, softly sensual way, which seemed to imply that he...that she...?

'You do? You never said anything about knowing Oliver to me, Lisa,' Henry said almost hectoringly.

But before Lisa could make any attempt to defend herself or explain Oliver Davenport was doing it for her, addressing Henry in a tone that left Lisa in no doubt as to just what kind of opinion the other man had of her husband-to-be, as he announced cuttingly, 'No doubt she had more important things on her mind. Or perhaps she simply didn't think it was important...'

'I...I...I didn't realise you two knew one another,' was the only response Lisa could come up with, and she saw from Henry's face that it was not really one that satisfied him.

She nibbled worriedly at her bottom lip, cast Oliver Davenport a bitter look and then was forced to listen helplessly whilst Oliver, who still quite obviously bore her a grudge over the clothes, commented judiciously, 'I like the outfit... It suits you... But then I thought so the first time I saw you wearing it, didn't I?'

Lisa knew that she was blushing. Blushing...? She was turning a vivid and unconcealable shade of deep scarlet, she acknowledged miserably as she saw the suspicious look that Henry was giving her and recognised from the narrow, pursed-lip glare that Henry's mother must have also overheard Oliver's comment.

'Oliver, let me get you a drink,' Henry's father offered, thankfully coming up to usher him away, but not before Oliver managed to murmur softly to Lisa,

'Saved by the cavalry...'

'How on earth do you come to know Oliver Davenport?' Henry demanded angrily as soon as Oliver was out of earshot.

'I don't *know* him,' Lisa admitted wearily. 'At least not—'

'What do you mean? Of course you *know* him...and well enough for him to be able to comment on your clothes...'

'He's... Henry...this isn't the time for me to explain...' Lisa told him quietly.

'So there *is* something to explain, then.' Henry was refusing to be appeased. 'Where did you meet him? In London, I suppose. His business might be based up here at the Hall, but he still spends quite a considerable amount of time in London... His cousin works for him down there—'

'His cousin...?' Lisa couldn't quite keep the note of nervous apprehension out of her voice.

'Yes, Piers Davenport, Oliver's cousin. He's several years younger than Oliver and he lives in London with his girlfriend—some model or other...Emily...or Emma...I can't remember which...'

'Emma,' Lisa supplied hollowly.

So Oliver hadn't been lying, after all, when he had told her that he was acting on behalf of his cousin. She glanced uneasily over her shoulder, remembering just exactly how scathingly she had denounced him, practically accusing him of being a liar and worse.

No wonder he had given her that look this evening which had said that he hadn't finished with her and that he fully intended to make her pay for her angry insults, to exact retribution on her.

Apprehensively she wondered exactly what form that silently promised retribution was going to take. What was he going to do? Reveal to Henry and his parents that she had bought her clothes second-hand? She could just imagine how Mary Hanford would react to that information. At the thought of her impending humiliation, Lisa felt her stomach muscles tighten defensively.

It wasn't all her fault. Hers had been a natural enough mistake to make, she reminded herself. Alison had agreed with her. And Oliver had to share some of the blame for her error himself. If he had only been a little more conciliatory in his manner towards her, a little less arrogant in demanding that she return the clothes back to him...

'I do wish you had told me that you knew Oliver,' Henry was continuing fussily. 'Especially in view of his position locally.'

'What position locally?' Lisa asked him warily, but she suspected she could guess the answer. To judge from Mary Hanford's deferential manner towards him, Oliver Davenport was quite obviously someone of importance in the area. Her heart started to sink even further as Henry explained in a hushed, almost awed voice.

'Oliver is an extremely wealthy man. He owns and runs one of the north of England's largest financial consultancy businesses and he recently took over another firm based in London, giving him a countrywide network. But why are you asking me? Surely if you know him you must—?'

'I don't know him,' Lisa protested tiredly. 'Henry, there's something I have to tell you.' She took a deep breath. There was nothing else for it; she was going to have to tell Henry the truth.

'But you evidently do know him,' Henry protested, ignoring her and cutting across what she was trying to say. 'And rather well by the sound of it... Lisa, what exactly's going on?'

Henry could look remarkably like his mother when he pursed his lips and narrowed his eyes like that, Lisa decided. She suddenly had a mental image of the children they might have together—little replicas of their grandmother. Quickly she banished the unwelcome vision.

'Henry, nothing is going on. If you would just let me explain—' Lisa began.

But once again she was interrupted, this time by Henry's mother, who bore down on them, placing a proprietorial hand on Henry's arm as she told him, 'Henry, dear, Aunt Elspeth wants to talk to you. She's over there by the French windows. She's brought her god-daughter with her. You remember Louise. You used to play together when you were children—such a sweet girl...'

To Lisa's chagrin, Henry was borne off by his mother, leaving her standing alone, nursing an unwanted glass of too sweet sherry.

What should have been the happiest Christmas Eve of her adult life was turning out to be anything but, she admitted gloomily as she watched a petite, doe-eyed brunette, presumably Aunt Elspeth's god-daughter, simpering up at a Henry who was quite plainly wallowing in her dewy-eyed, fascinated attention.

It was a good thirty minutes before Henry returned to her side, during which time she had had ample opportunity to watch Oliver's progress amongst the guests and to wonder why on earth he had accepted the Hanfords' invitation, since he was quite obviously both bored and irritated by the almost fawning attention of Henry's mother.

He really was the most arrogantly supercilious man she had ever had the misfortune to meet, Lisa decided critically as he caught her watching him and lifted one derogatory, darkly interrogative eyebrow in her direction.

Flushing, she turned away, but not, she noticed, before Henry's mother had seen the brief, silent exchange between them.

'You still haven't explained to us just how you come to know... You really should have told us that you know Oliver,' she told Lisa, arriving at her side virtually at the same time as Henry, so that Lisa was once again prevented from explaining to him what had happened.

What was it about some people that made everything they said sound like either a reproach or a criticism? Lisa wondered grimly, but before she could answer she heard Mary Hanford adding, in an unfamiliar, almost arch and flattering voice, 'Ah, Oliver, we were just talking about you.'

'Really.'

He was looking at them contemptuously, as though they were creatures from another planet—some kind of subspecies provided for his entertainment, Lisa decided resentfully as he looked from Mary to Henry and then to her.

'Yes,' Mary continued, undeterred. 'I was just asking Lisa how she comes to know you...'

'Well, I think that's probably best left for Lisa herself to explain to you,' he responded smoothly. 'I should hate to embarrass her by making any unwelcome revelations...'

Lisa glared angrily at him.

'That suit looks good on you,' he added softly.

'So you've already said,' she reminded him through gritted teeth, all too aware of Henry and his mother's silently suspicious watchfulness at her side.

'Yes,' Oliver continued, as though she hadn't spoken. 'You can always tell when a woman's wearing an outfit bought by a man for his lover.' As he spoke he reached out and touched her jacket-clad arm—a brief touch, nothing more, but it made the hot colour burn in Lisa's face, and she was not at all surprised to hear Henry's mother's outraged indrawn breath or to see the fury in Henry's eyes.

This was retribution with a vengeance. This wasn't just victory, she acknowledged helplessly; it was total annihilation.

'Have you worn any of the other things yet?' he added casually.

'Lisa...' she heard Henry demanding ominously at her side, but she couldn't answer him. She was too mortified, too furiously angry to dare to risk saying anything whilst Oliver Davenport was still standing there listening.

To her relief, he didn't linger long. Aunt Elspeth's god-daughter, the same one who had so determinedly flirted with Henry half an hour earlier, came up and very professionally broke up their quartet, insisting that Oliver had promised to get her a fresh drink.

He was barely out of earshot before Henry was insisting, 'I want to know what's going on, Lisa... What was all that about your clothes...?'

'I think we know exactly what's going on, Henry,' Lisa heard his mother answering coolly for him as she gave Lisa a look of virulent hostility edged with triumph. So much for pretending to welcome her into the family, Lisa thought tiredly.

'I can see what you're *both* thinking,' she announced. 'But you are wrong.'

'Wrong? How can we be wrong when Oliver more or less announced openly that the pair of you have been lovers?' Mary intoned.

'He did not announce that we had been lovers,' Lisa defended herself. 'And if you would just let me explain—'

'Henry, it's almost time for supper. You know how hopeless your father is at getting people organised. I'm going to need you to help me...'

'Henry, we need to talk.' Lisa tried to override his mother, but Henry was already turning away from her and going obediently to his mother's side.

If they married it would always be like this, Lisa suddenly recognised on a wave of helpless anger. He would always place his mother's needs and wants above her own, and presumably above those of their children. They would always come a very poor second best to his loyalty to his mother. Was that really what she wanted for herself... for her children?

Lisa knew it wasn't.

It was as though the scales had suddenly fallen from her eyes, as though she were looking at a picture of exactly how and what her life with Henry would be—and she didn't like it. She didn't like it one little bit.

In the handful of seconds it took her to recognise the fact, she knew irrevocably that she couldn't marry him, but she still owed him an explanation of what had happened, and from her own point of view. For the sake of her pride and self-respect she wanted to make sure that he and his precious mother knew exactly how she had come to meet Oliver and exactly how he had manipulated them into believing his deliberately skewed view of the situation.

Still seething with anger against Oliver, she refused Henry's father's offer of another drink and some supper.

She would choke rather than eat any of Mary Hanford's food, she decided angrily.

Just the thought of the kind of life she would have had as Henry's wife made her shudder and acknowledge that she had had a lucky escape, but knowing that did not lessen her overwhelming fury at the man who had accidently brought it about.

How would she have been feeling right now had she been deeply in love with Henry and he with her? Instead of stalking angrily around the Hanfords' drawing room like an angry tigress, she would probably have been upstairs in her bedroom sobbing her heart out.

Some Christmas this was going to be.

She had been so looking forward to being here, to being part of the family, to sharing the simple, traditional pleasures of Christmas with the man she intended to marry, and now it was all spoiled, ruined... And why? Why? Because Oliver Davenport was too arrogant, too proud... too... too devious and hateful to allow someone whom he obviously saw as way, way beneath him to get the better of him.

Well, she didn't care. She didn't care what he did or what he said. He could tell the whole room, the whole house, the whole world that she had bought her clothes second-hand and that they had belonged to his cousin's girlfriend for all she cared now. In fact, she almost wished he would. That way at least she would be vindicated. That way she could walk away from here...from Henry and his precious mother...with her head held high.

'An outfit bought by a man for his lover...' How dared he...? Oh, how dared he...? She was, she suddenly realised, almost audibly grinding her teeth. Hastily she stopped. Dental fees were notoriously, hideously expensive.

She couldn't leave matters as they were, she decided fiercely. She would have to say something to Oliver Davenport—even if it was to challenge him over the implications he had made.

She got her chance ten minutes later, when she saw Oliver leaving the drawing room alone.

Quickly, before she could change her mind, she followed him. As he heard her footsteps crossing the hallway, he stopped and turned round.

'Ah, the blushing bride-to-be and her borrowed raiment,' he commented sardonically.

'I bought in good faith my second-hand raiment,' Lisa corrected him bitingly, adding, 'You do realise what impression you gave Henry and his mother back there, don't you?' she challenged him, adding scornfully before he could answer, 'Of course you knew. You knew perfectly well what you were doing, what you were implying...'

'Did I?' he responded calmly.

'Yes, you did,' Lisa responded, her anger intensifying. 'You knew they would assume that you meant that you and I had been lovers... that *you* had bought my clothes—'

'Surely Henry knows you far better than that?' Oliver interrupted her smoothly. 'After all, according to the local grapevine, the pair of you are intending to marry—'

'Of course Henry knows me...' Lisa began, and then stopped, her face flushing in angry mortification. But it was too late.

Swift as a hawk to the lure, her tormentor responded softly, 'Ah, I see. It's because he knows you so well that he made the unfortunate and mistaken assumption that—'

'No... He doesn't... I don't...' Lisa tried to fight back gamely, but it was still too late, and infuriatingly she knew it and, even worse, so did Oliver.

He wasn't smirking precisely—he was far too arrogant for that, Lisa decided bitterly—but there was certainly mockery in his eyes, and if she hadn't known better she could almost have sworn that his mouth was about to curl into a smile—but how could it? She was sure that he was incapable of doing anything so human. He was the kind of man who just didn't know what human emotions were, she decided savagely—who had no idea what it meant to suffer insecurity or... or any of the things that made people like herself feel so vulnerable.

'Have you any idea what you've done?' she challenged him, changing tack, her voice shaking under the weight of her suppressed emotion. 'I came here—'

'I know why you came here,' he interrupted her with unexpected sternness. 'You came to be looked over as a potential wife for Mary Hanford's precious son.

'Where's your pride?' he demanded scornfully. 'However, a potential bride is all you will ever be. Mary Hanford knows quite well who she wants Henry to marry, and I'm afraid it isn't going to be you...'

'Not now,' Lisa agreed shortly. 'Not—'

'Not ever,' Oliver told her. 'Mary won't allow Henry to marry any woman who she thinks might have the slightest chance of threatening her own superior position in Henry's life. His wife will not only have to take second place to her but to covertly acknowledge and accept that fact before she's allowed to marry him. And besides, the two of you are so obviously unsuited to one another that the whole thing's almost a farce. You're far too emotionally turbulent and uncontrolled for Henry... He wouldn't have a clue how to handle you...'

Lisa couldn't believe her ears.

'You, of course, would,' she challenged him with acid sweetness, too carried away by her anger and the heat of the moment to realise what she was doing, the challenge she was issuing him, the risks she was taking.

Then it was too late and he was cutting the ground from beneath her feet and making a shock as icy-cold as the snow melting on the tops of the Yorkshire hills that were his home run down her spine as he told her silkily, 'Certainly,' and then added before she could draw breath to speak, 'And, for openers, there are two things I most certainly would do that Henry obviously has not.'

'Oh, yes, and what exactly would they be?' Lisa demanded furiously.

'Well, I certainly wouldn't have the kind of relationship with you—or with any woman who I had the slightest degree of mild affection for, never mind being on the point of contemplating marrying—which would necessitate you feeling that you had to conceal anything about yourself from me, or that you needed to impress my family and friends with borrowed plumes, with the contents of another woman's wardrobe. And the second...' he continued, ignoring Lisa's quick, indrawn breath of mingled chagrin and rage.

He paused and looked at her whilst Lisa, driven well beyond the point of no return by the whole farce of her ruined Christmas in general and his part in it in particular, prompted wildly, 'Yes, the second is...?'

'This,' he told her softly, taking the breath from her lungs, the strength from her muscles and, along with them, the will-power from her brain as he stepped forward and took her in his arms and then bent his head and kissed her as Henry had never kissed her in all the eight months of their relationship—as no man had ever kissed her in the whole history of her admittedly modest sexual experience, she recognised dizzily as his mouth moved with unbelievable, unbeatable, unbearable sensual expertise on hers.

Ordinary mortal men did not kiss like this. Ordinary mortal men did not behave like this. Ordinary mortal men did not have the power, did not cup one's face with such tender mastery. They did not look deep into your eyes whilst they caressed your mouth with their own. They did not compel you, by some mastery you could not understand, to look back at them. They did not, by some unspoken command, cause you to open your mouth beneath theirs on a whispered ecstatic sigh of pure female pleasure. They did not lift their mouths from yours and look from your eyes to your half-parted lips and then back to your eyes again, their own warming in a smile of complicit understanding before starting to kiss you all over again.

Film stars in impossibly extravagant and highly acclaimed, Oscar-winning romantic movies might mimic such behaviour. Heroes in stomach-churning, body-aching, romantically sensual novels might sweep their heroines off their feet with similar embraces. God-like creatures from Greek mythology might come down to earth and wantonly seduce frolicking nymphs with such devastating experience and sensuality, but mere mortal men...? Never!

Lisa gave a small, blissful sigh and closed her eyes, only to open them again as she heard Henry exclaiming wrathfully, 'Lisa...what on earth do you think you're doing?'

Guiltily she watched him approaching as Oliver released her.

'Henry, I can explain,' she told him urgently, but he obviously didn't intend to let her speak.

Ignoring Oliver's quiet voice mocking, 'To Henry, maybe, but to Mary, never,' she flushed defensively as his taunting comment was borne out by Henry's furious declaration.

'Mother was right about you all along. She warned me that you weren't—'

'Henry, you don't understand.' She managed to interrupt him, turning to appeal to Oliver, who was standing watching them in contemptuous amusement.

'Tell him what really happened ... Tell him ...'

'Do you really expect me to give you my help?' he goaded her softly. 'I don't recall you being similarly sympathetic when I asked you for yours.'

Whilst Lisa stood and stared at him in disbelief he started to walk towards the door, pausing only to tell Henry, 'Your mother is quite right, Henry. She wouldn't be the right wife for you at all ... If I were you I should heed her advice—now, before it's too late.'

'Henry,' Lisa began to protest, but she could see from the way that he was refusing to meet her eyes that she had lost what little chance she might have had of persuading him to listen to her.

'It's too late now for us to change our plans for Christmas,' he told her stiffly, still avoiding looking directly at her. 'It is, after all, Christmas Eve, and we can hardly ask you to... However, once we return to London I feel that it would be as well if we didn't see one another any more ...'

Lisa could scarcely believe her ears. Was this really the man she had thought she loved, or had at least liked and admired enough to be her husband ... the man she had wanted as the father of her children? This pompous, stuffy creature who preferred to take his mother's advice on whom he should and should not marry than to listen to her, the woman he had proclaimed he loved?

Only he had not—not really, had he? Lisa made herself admit honestly. Neither of them had really truly been in love. Oh, they had liked one another well enough. But liking wasn't love, and if she was honest with herself there was a strong chord of relief mixed up in the turbulent anger and resentment churning her insides.

Stay here now, over Christmas, after what had happened . . .? No way.

Without trusting herself to speak to Henry, she turned on her heel and headed for the stairs and her bedroom, where she threw open the wardrobe doors and started to remove her clothes—her borrowed clothes, not her clothes, she acknowledged grimly as she opened her suitcase; they hadn't been hers when she had bought them and they certainly weren't hers now.

Eyeing them with loathing, her attention was momentarily distracted by the damp chilliness of her bedroom. Thank goodness they had driven north in her car. At least she wasn't going to have the added humiliation of depending on Henry to get her back to London.

The temperature seemed to have dropped since she had left the bedroom earlier, even taking into account Mary Hanford's parsimony.

There had been another warning of snow on high ground locally earlier in the evening, and Lisa had been enchanted by it, wondering out loud if they might actually have a white Christmas—a long-held childhood wish of hers which she had so far never had fulfilled. Mary Hanford had been scornful of her excitement.

As she gathered up her belongings Lisa suddenly paused; the clothes she had bought with such pleasure and which she had held onto with such determination lay on the bed in an untidy heap.

Beautiful though they were, she suddenly felt that she knew now that she could never wear them. They were tainted. Some things were just not meant to be, she decided regretfully as she stroked the silk fabric of one of the shirts with tender fingers.

She might have paid for them, bought them in all good faith, but somehow she had never actually felt as though they were hers.

But it was her borrowed clothes, like the borrowed persona she had perhaps unwittingly tried to assume to impress Henry's family, which had proved her downfall, and she was, she decided firmly, better off without both of them.

Ten minutes later, wearing her own jeans, she lifted the carefully folded clothes into her suitcase. Once the Christmas holiday was over she would telephone the dress agency and explain that she no longer had any use for the clothes. Hopefully they would be prepared to take them back and refund most, if not all of her money.

It was too late to regret now that she had not accepted Alison's suggestion that she join her and some other friends on a Christmas holiday and skiing trip to Colorado. Christmas was going to be very lonely for her alone in her flat with all her friends and her parents away. A sadly wistful smile curved the generous softness of her mouth as she contemplated how very different from her rosy daydreams the reality of her Christmas was going to be.

'You're going to the north of England—Yorkshire. I know it has a reputation for being much colder up there than it is here in London, but that doesn't mean you'll get snow,' Alison had warned her, adding more gently, 'Don't invest too much in this visit to Henry's family, Lisa. I know how important it is to you but things don't always work out the way you plan. The Yorkshire Dales are a beautiful part of the world, but people are still people and—well, let's face it, from what Henry has said about his family, especially his mother, it's obvious that she's inclined to be a little on the possessive side.'

'I know you don't really like Henry...' Lisa had begun defensively.

But Alison had shaken her head and told her firmly, 'It isn't that I don't care for Henry, rather that I *do* care about you. He isn't right for you, Lisa. Oh, I know what you're going to say: he's solid and dependable, and with him you can put down the roots that are so important to you. But, to be honest—well, if you want the truth, I see Henry more as a rather spoiled little boy than the kind of man a woman can rely on.'

It looked as if Alison was a much better judge of character than she, Lisa acknowledged as she zipped her case shut and picked it up.

CHAPTER THREE

LISA was halfway down the stairs when Henry walked into the hallway and saw her.

'Lisa, why are you dressed like that? Where are you going?' he demanded as he looked anxiously back over his shoulder, obviously not wanting anyone else to witness what was going on.

'I'm leaving,' she told him calmly. It was odd that she should be able to remain so calm with Henry who, after all, until this evening's debacle had been the man she had intended to marry, the man she had planned to spend the rest of her life with, and yet with Oliver, a complete stranger, a man she had seen only twice before and whom she expected . . . hoped . . . she would never see again, her emotions became inflamed into a rage of gargantuan proportions.

'Leaving? But you can't . . . What will people think?' Henry protested. 'Mother's got the whole family coming for Christmas dinner tomorrow and they'll all expect you to be there. We were, after all, planning to announce our engagement,' he reminded her seriously.

As she listened to him in disbelief Lisa was shocked to realise that she badly wanted to laugh—or cry.

'Henry, I can't stay here now,' she told him. 'Not after what's happened. You must see that. After all you were the one—'

'You're leaving to go to him, aren't you?' Henry accused her angrily. 'Well, don't expect Oliver to offer to marry you, Lisa. He might want to take you to bed but,

48

as Mother says, Oliver isn't the kind of man to marry a woman who—'

That was it. Suddenly Lisa had had enough. Her face flushing with the full force of her emotions, she descended the last few stairs and confronted Henry.

'I don't care what your mother says, Henry,' she told him through gritted teeth. 'And if you were half the man I thought you were *you* wouldn't care either. Neither would you let her make up your mind or your decisions for you... And as for Oliver—'

'Yes, as for me... what?'

To her consternation Lisa realised that at some point Oliver had walked into the hall and was now standing watching them both, an infuriatingly superior, mocking contempt curling his mouth as he broke into her angry tirade.

'I've had enough of this... I've had enough of both of you,' Lisa announced. 'This is all your fault. All of it,' she added passionately to Oliver, ignoring Henry's attempts to silence her.

'And don't think I haven't guessed why you've done it,' she added furiously, her fingers tugging at the strap of her suitcase. She wrenched the case open and cried out angrily to him, 'You want your precious clothes back? Well, you can have them... all of them...'

Fiercely she wrenched the carefully packed clothes from her case and hurled them across the small space that lay between them, where they landed in an untidy heap at Oliver's feet.

She ignored Henry's anguished, shocked, 'Lisa...what on earth are you doing...? Lisa, please...stop; someone might see... Mother...'

'Oh, and we mustn't forget this, must we?' Lisa continued, ignoring Henry, an almost orgasmic feeling of release drowning out all her normal level-headedness and common sense. For the first time in her life she could understand why it was some people actually seemed to enjoy losing their temper, giving up their self-control...causing a scene...all things that were normally completely foreign to her.

Triumphantly she threw the beautiful Armani suit which she had bought with such pleasure at Oliver's feet whilst he watched her impassively.

'There! I hope you're satisfied,' she told him as the last garment headed his way.

'Lisa,' Henry was still bleating protestingly, but she ignored him. Now that the sudden, unfamiliar surge of anger was retreating she felt oddly weak and shaky, almost vulnerably light-headed and dangerously close to tears.

In the distance she was aware that Henry was still protesting, but for some reason it was Oliver whom her attention was concentrated on, who filled her vision and her prickly, wary senses as she deliberately skirted around him, clutching her still half-open but now much lighter suitcase, and headed for the front door.

There had been a look in his eyes as she had flung that trouser suit at him which she had not totally understood—a gleam of an emotion which in another man she could almost have felt was humour mixed with a certain rueful respect, but of course she must have been imagining it.

As she tugged open the front door and stepped outside a shock of ice-cold air hit her. She hadn't realised how much the temperature had dropped, how overcast the sky had become.

Frost crunched beneath her feet as she hurried towards her car. Faithful and reliable as ever, it started at the second turn of the key.

As Lisa negotiated the other cars parked in the drive she told herself grimly that she had no need to try to work out whom that gleaming, shiny Aston Martin sports car belonged to. It just had to be Oliver Davenport's.

As she turned onto the main road she switched on her car radio, her heart giving a small forlorn thud of regret as she heard the announcer forecasting that the north of England was due to have snow.

Snow for Christmas and she was going to miss it.

It was half past eleven; another half an hour and it would be Christmas Day, and she would be spending it alone.

Stop snivelling, she told herself as she felt her throat start to ache with emotional tears. You've had a lucky escape.

She knew she had a fairly long drive ahead of her before she reached the motorway. As she and Henry had driven north she had remarked on how beautiful the countryside was as they drove through it. Now, however, as she drove along the empty, dark country road she was conscious of how remote the area was and how alone she felt.

She frowned as the car engine started to splutter and lose power, anxiety tensing her body as she wondered what on earth was wrong. Her small car had always been so reliable, and she was very careful about having it properly serviced and keeping the tank full of petrol.

Petrol. Lisa knew what had happened from the sharp sinking sensation in her stomach even before she looked fearfully at the petrol gauge.

Henry had not bothered to replace the petrol they had used on the journey north and now, it seemed, the tank was empty.

Lisa closed her eyes in mute despair. What on earth was she going to do? She was stranded on an empty country road miles from anywhere in the dark on Christmas Eve, with no idea where the nearest garage was, no means of contacting anyone to ask, dressed in jeans and a thin sweater on a freezing cold night.

And she knew exactly who she had to blame for her sorry plight, she decided wrathfully ten minutes later as the air inside her car turned colder and colder with ominous speed. Oliver Davenport. If it hadn't been for him and his cynical and deliberate manipulation of the truth to cast her in a bad light in front of Henry and his parents, none of this would have happened.

Even now she still couldn't quite believe what she had done in the full force of that final, unexpected burst of temper, when she had thrown her clothes at him.

Lisa hugged her arms tightly around her body as she started to shiver. It was too late to regret her hasty departure from Henry's parents' home now, or the fact that she had brought nothing with her that she could use to keep her warm.

Just how far was it to the nearest house? Her teeth were chattering now and the windscreen had started to freeze over.

Perhaps she ought to start walking back in the direction she had come. At least then the physical activity might help to keep her warm, but her heart sank at the thought. So far as she could remember, she had been driving for a good fifteen minutes after she had passed through the last small hamlet, and she hadn't seen any houses since then.

Reluctantly she opened the car door, and then closed it again with a gasp of shock as the ice-cold wind knifed into her unprotected body.

What on earth was she going to do? Her earlier frustration and irritation had started to give way to a far more ominous and much deeper sense of panicky fear.

One read about people being found dying from exposure and hypothermia, but it always seemed such an unreal fate somehow in a country like Britain. Now, though, it suddenly seemed horribly plausible.

Her panic intensified as she realised that unless she either managed to walk to the nearest inhabited building, wherever that might be, or was spotted by a passing motorist, it would be days before anyone realised that she was missing. There was, after all, no one waiting at home in London for her. Her parents had agreed not to telephone on Christmas Day because they knew she would be staying with Henry's family. Henry would assume—if indeed he gave her any thought at all—that she was back in London.

As she fought down the emotions threatening to overwhelm her Lisa happened to glance at her watch.

It was almost half past twelve . . . Christmas Day.

Now she couldn't stop the tears.

Christmas Day and she was stuck in a car miles from anywhere and probably about to freeze to death.

She gave a small, protesting moan as she sneezed and then sneezed again, blinking her eyes against the dazzling glare of headlights she could see in her driving mirror.

The dazzling glare of headlights . . . Another car . . .

Frantically Lisa pushed on her frozen car door, terrified that her unwitting rescuer might drive past her without realising her plight.

The approaching car was only yards behind her when she finally managed to shove open the door. As she half fell into the icy road in her haste to advertise her predicament any thoughts of the danger of flagging down a stranger were completely forgotten in the more overriding urgency of her plight.

The dazzle of the oncoming headlights was so powerful that she couldn't distinguish the shape of the car or see its driver, but she knew he or she had seen her because the car suddenly started to lose speed, swerving to a halt in front of her.

Now that the car was stationary Lisa recognised that there was something vaguely familiar about it, but her relief overrode that awareness as she ran towards it on legs which suddenly seemed as stiff and wobbly as those of a newborn colt.

However, before she could reach it, the driver's door was flung open and a pair of long male legs appeared, followed by an equally imposing and stomach-churningly recognisable male torso and face.

As she stared disbelievingly into the frowning, impatient face of Oliver Davenport, Lisa protested fatalistically, 'Oh, no, not you...'

'Who were you hoping it was—Henry?' he retorted sardonically. 'If this is your idea of staging a reconciliation scene, I have to tell you that you're wasting your time. When I left him you were the last thing on Henry's mind.'

'Of course I'm not staging a reconciliation scene,' Lisa snapped back at him. 'I'm not staging a scene of any kind... I—it isn't something I do...'

The effect of her cool speech was unfairly spoiled by the sudden fit of shivering that overtook her, but it was plain that Oliver Davenport wouldn't have been very impressed with it anyway because he drawled, 'Oh, no? Then what was all that highly theatrical piece of overacting in the Hanfords' hall all about?'

'That wasn't overacting,' Lisa gritted at him. 'That was...'

She shivered again, this time so violently that her teeth chattered audibly.

'For God's sake, put a coat on. Have you any idea what the temperature is tonight? I know you're from the south and a city, but surely common sense—?'

'I don't have a coat,' Lisa told him, adding bitterly, 'Because of you.'

The look he gave her was incredulously contemptuous.

'Are you crazy? You come north in the middle of December and you don't even bother to bring a coat—'

'Oh, I brought a coat all right,' Lisa corrected him between shivers. 'Only I don't have it now...'

She gritted her teeth and tried not to think about the warmth of the lovely, heavenly cream cashmere coat which had been amongst the things she had thrown at his feet so recklessly.

'You don't... Ah... I see... What are you doing, anyway? Why have you stopped?'

'Why do you think I've stopped? Not to admire the view,' Lisa told him bitterly. 'The car's run out of petrol.'

'The car's run out of petrol?'

Lisa felt herself flushing as she heard the disbelieving male scorn in his voice.

'It wasn't my fault,' she defended herself. 'We were supposed to be coming north in Henry's car, only it was involved in an accident and couldn't be driven so we had to use mine, and Henry was so anxious to get... not to be late that he didn't want to stop and refill the tank...'

Lisa hated the way he was just standing silently looking at her. He was determined to make things as hard for her as he could. She could see that... He was positively enjoying making her look small... humiliating her.

In any other circumstances but these she would have been tempted simply to turn her back on him, get back in her car and wait for the next driver to come by, but common sense warned her that she couldn't afford to take that kind of risk.

Her unprotected fingers had already turned white and were almost numb. She couldn't feel her toes, and the rest of her body felt so cold that the sensation was almost a physical pain.

Taking a deep breath and fixing her gaze on a point just beyond his left shoulder, she said shakily, 'I'd be very grateful if you could give me a lift to the nearest garage...'

Tensely she waited for his response, knowing that he was bound to make the most of the opportunity which she had given him to exercise his obvious dislike of her. But when it came the blow was one of such magnitude and such force that she physically winced beneath the cruelty of it, the breath escaping from her lungs in a soft, shocked gasp as he told her ruthlessly, 'No way.'

It must be the cold that was making her feel so dizzy and light-headed, Lisa thought despairingly—that and her panicky fear that he was going to walk away and simply leave her here to meet her fate.

Whatever the cause, it propelled her into instinctive action, making her dart forward and catch hold of the fabric of his jacket as she told him jerkily, 'It wasn't *my* fault that your cousin sold his girlfriend's clothes without her permission. All *I* did was buy them in good faith... He's the one you should be punishing, not me. If you leave me here—'

'*Leave* you here...?'

Somehow or other he had detached her hand from his jacket and was now holding it in his own. Dizzily Lisa marvelled at how warm and comforting, how strong and safe it felt to have that large male hand enclosing hers. She could almost feel the warmth from his touch—his body—flooding up through her arm like an infusion of life-giving blood into a vein.

'Leave you *here* in this temperature?' he said, adding roughly, 'Are you crazy...?'

She couldn't see him properly any more, Lisa realised, and she thought it must be because the tears that had threatened her eyes had frozen in the intense cold. She had no idea that she had actually spoken her sentiments out loud until she heard him respond, 'Tears don't freeze; they're saline...salty.'

He had let go of her hand and as Lisa watched him he stripped off his jacket and then, to her shock, took hold of her and bundled her up in it like an adult wrapping up a small child.

'I can't walk,' she protested, her voice muffled by the thickness of the over-large wrapping.

'You're not going to,' she was told peremptorily, and then, before she knew what was happening, he was picking her up and carrying her the short distance to his car, opening the passenger door and depositing her on the seat.

The car smelled of leather and warmth and something much more intangible—something elusive and yet oddly familiar... Muzzily Lisa sniffed, trying to work out what it was and why it should inexplicably make her want to cry and yet at the same time feel oddly elated.

Oliver had gone over to her car, and as he returned Lisa saw that he was carrying her case and her handbag.

'I've locked it...your car,' he told her as he slid into the driver's seat alongside her. 'Not that anyone would be likely to take it.'

'Not unless they had some petrol with them,' Lisa agreed drowsily, opening her mouth to give a yawn which suddenly turned into a volley of bone-aching sneezes.

'Here.' Oliver handed her a wad of clean tissues from a pack in the glove compartment, telling her, 'It's just as well I happened to be passing when I did. If you're lucky the worst you'll suffer is a bad cold; another hour in these temperatures and it could have been a very different story. This road is never very heavily trafficked, and on Christmas Eve, with snow forecast, the locals who do use it have more sense than to...'

He went on talking but Lisa had heard enough. Did he think she had wanted to run out of petrol on a remote Yorkshire road? Had he forgotten whose fault it was that she had been there in the first place instead of warmly tucked up in bed at Henry's parents' home?

Tears of unfamiliar and unexpected self-pity suddenly filled her eyes. 'It isn't Christmas Eve,' she told him aggressively, fighting to hold them back. 'It's Christmas Day.'

It was the wrong thing to say, bringing back her earlier awareness of how very fragile were the brightly coloured, delicate daydreams that she had cherished of how this Christmas would be—as fragile and vulnerable as the glass baubles with which she had so foolishly imagined herself decorating that huge, freshly cut, pine-smelling Christmas tree with Henry.

It was too much. One tear fell and then another. She tried to stop them, dabbing surreptitiously at her eyes, and she averted her face from Oliver's as he started the engine and set the car in motion. But it was no use. He had obviously witnessed her distress.

'Now what's wrong?' he demanded grimly.

'It's Christmas Day,' Lisa wept.

'Christmas Day.' He repeated the words as though he had never heard them before. 'Where would you have been spending it if your car hadn't run out of petrol?' he asked her. 'Where were you going?'

'Home to London, to my flat,' Lisa told him wearily. Despite the fact that at some point, without her being aware of it, he had obviously noticed that she was shivering and had turned the heater on full, she still felt frighteningly cold.

'My parents are both working away in Japan so I can't go to them, and my friends have made other plans. I could have gone with them, but...'

'But you chose to subject yourself to Henry's mother's inspection instead,' he taunted her unkindly.

'Henry and I were planning to get engaged,' Lisa fought back angrily. 'Of course he wanted me to meet his parents, his family. There was no question of there being any "inspection".'

'No? Then why the urgent necessity for a new wardrobe?'

Lisa flushed defensively.

'I just wanted to make a good impression on them, that's all,' she muttered.

'Well, you certainly did that all right,' he mocked her wryly. 'Especially—'

'I would have done if it hadn't been for your interference,' she interrupted him hotly. 'You had no right to imply that you and I had been...that those clothes...' She paused, her voice trailing away into silence as she saw the way he lifted one eyebrow and glanced unkindly at her.

'I spoke nothing but the truth. Those clothes were bought by my cousin for his girlfriend—his lover...'

'It might have been the truth, but you twisted it so that it seemed ... so that it sounded ... so that...'

Lisa floundered, her face flushing betrayingly as he invited helpfully, 'So that what?'

'So that people would think that you and I...that you had bought those clothes for me and that you and I were lovers,' she told him fiercely.

'But surely anyone who really knows you...a prospective fiancé, an established lover, for instance...would automatically know that it was impossible for us to be lovers?' he pointed out to her.

'Henry and I are not lovers.'

Lisa bit her lip in vexation. Now what on earth had prompted her to tell him that? It was hardly the sort of thing she would normally discuss with someone who was virtually a stranger.

Again the dark eyebrows rose—both of them this time—his response to her admission almost brutally comprehensive as he asked her crisply, 'You're not? Then what on earth were you doing thinking of getting engaged to him?'

Lisa opened her mouth but the words she wanted to say simply wouldn't come. How could she say them now? How could she tell him, I loved him, when she knew irrevocably and blindingly that it simply wasn't true, that it had possibly and shamingly never been true and that, just as shamingly, she had somehow managed to delude herself that it might be and to convince herself that she and Henry had a future together?

In the end she had to settle for a stiff and totally unconvincing, 'It seemed a good idea at the time. We had a lot in common. We were both ready to settle down, to commit ourselves. To—' She stopped speaking as the sound of his laughter suddenly filled the car, drowning out the sound of her own voice.

He had a very full, deep, rich-bodied and very male laugh, she acknowledged—a very...a very...a very sensual, sexy sort of laugh...if you cared for that sort of thing...and of course she didn't, she reminded herself firmly.

'Why are you laughing?' she demanded angrily, her cheeks flying hot banners of scorching colour as she turned in her seat to glare furiously at him. 'It isn't...there isn't anything to laugh at...'

'No, there isn't,' he agreed soberly. 'You're right... By rights I— How old are you? What century are you living in? "We had a lot in common. We were both ready to settle down..."' he mimicked her. 'Even if that was true, which it quite patently is not—in fact, I doubt I've ever seen a couple more obviously totally unsuited to one another—I have never heard of a less convincing reason for wanting to get married.

'Why haven't you been to bed with him?' he demanded, the unexpectedness of the question shocking her, taking her breath away.

'I don't think that's any of your business,' she told him primly.

'Which one of you was it who didn't want to—you or him?'

Lisa gasped, outraged. 'Not everyone has...has a high sex drive...or wants a...a relationship that's based on...on physical lust,' she told him angrily. 'And just because...'

Whilst they had been talking Oliver had been driving, and now unexpectedly he turned off the main road and in between two stone pillars into what was obviously the drive to a private house—a very long drive, Lisa noted, before turning towards him and demanding, 'What are you doing? Where are you taking me? This isn't a garage.'

'No, it isn't,' he agreed calmly. 'It's my home.'

'Your home? But—'

'Calm down,' Oliver advised her drily. 'Look, it's gone one in the morning, Christmas morning,' he emphasised. 'This isn't London; the nearest large petrol station is on the motorway, nearly thirty miles away, *if* it's open—and personally what I think you need right now more than anything else is a hot bath and a good night's sleep.'

'I want to go home,' Lisa insisted stubbornly.

'Why?' he challenged her brutally, and reminded her, 'You've already said yourself that there's no one there. Look,' he told her, 'since it is Christmas, why don't we declare a cease-fire in our...er...hostilities? Although by choice neither of us might have wanted to spend Christmas together, since we are both on our own and since it's patently obvious that you're in no physical state to go anywhere, never mind drive a car—'

'You're spending Christmas on your own?' Lisa interrupted him, too astonished to hold the question back.

'Yes,' he agreed, explaining, 'I was to have spent it entertaining my cousin and his girlfriend, but since they've made up their quarrel their plans have changed and they flew to the Caribbean yesterday morning. Like you, I'd left it too late to make alternative plans and so—'

'I can't stay with you,' Lisa protested. She was, she recognised, already starting to shiver as the now stationary car started to cool down, and she was also unpleasantly and weakly aware of how very unappealing the thought of driving all the way back to London actually was—and not just unappealing either, she admitted. She was uncomfortably conscious that Oliver had spoken the truth when he had claimed that she was not physically capable of making the journey at present.

'We're strangers...'

'You've already accepted a lift in my car,' he reminded her drily, adding pithily, 'And besides, where else can you go?'

All at once Lisa gave in. She really didn't have the energy to argue with him, she admitted—she was too cold, too tired, too muzzily aware of how dangerously light-headed and weak she was beginning to feel.

'Very well, then,' she said, adding warningly, 'But only until tomorrow... until I can get some petrol.'

'Only until tomorrow,' he agreed.

CHAPTER FOUR

'YOU live here all alone?' Lisa questioned Oliver, breaking into his conversation as she curled up in one corner of the vast, deep sofa where he had taken her and told her sternly she was to remain until he returned with a hot drink for her.

'Yes,' he said. 'I prefer it that way. A gardener comes twice a week and his wife does the cleaning for me, but other than that—'

'But it's such a big house. Don't you...?'

'Don't I what?' Oliver challenged her. 'Don't I feel lonely?' He shook his head. 'Not really. I was an only child. My mother died when I was in my teens and my father was away a lot on business. I'm used to being on my own. In fact I prefer it in many ways. Other people's company, their presence in one's life isn't always a pleasure—especially not when one has to become responsible for their emotional and financial welfare.'

Lisa guessed that he was referring obliquely to his cousin, and she sensed that he was, by nature, the kind of man who would always naturally assume responsibility for others, even if that responsibility was slightly irritably cynical rather than humanely compassionate. It also probably explained why he wasn't married. He was by nature a loner—a man, she suspected, who enjoyed women's company but who did not want to burden himself with a wife or children.

And yet a house like this cried out for children. It had that kind of ambience about it, that kind of warmth; it was a real family home for all its obviously priceless antiques. It had a lived-in, welcoming feel to it, Lisa acknowledged—a sense of having been well used and well loved, a slightly worn air which, to her, gave it a richness that far surpassed the sterile, elegant perfection of a house like Henry's parents'.

It didn't surprise Lisa to learn that the house had been in Oliver's family for several generations but what did surprise her was how at ease, how at home she actually felt here, how unexpectedly easy it was to talk to Oliver after he had returned from the kitchen with a huge mug of piping-hot chocolate which he insisted she drink, virtually standing over her until she had done so.

She had suspected from the taste of it that something very much more alcoholic than mere milk had been added to it, but by that stage she had been so grateful for the warmth of her comfortable niche in the deep sofa, so drowsily content and relaxed that there hadn't seemed to be any point in mentioning it, never mind protesting about it.

Now, as she yawned sleepily, blinking owlishly, her forehead pleating in a muzzy frown as she tried to focus on the fireplace and discovered that she couldn't, she was vaguely aware of Oliver getting up from his own chair and coming over to her, leaning down towards her as he firmly relieved her of the now empty mug.

'Bath for you, and then bed, I think,' he told her firmly, sounding so much as her father had when she had been a little girl that Lisa turned her head to look at him.

She hadn't realised that he was quite so close to her, nor that his grey eyes had a darker outer rim to them and were not flat, dead grey at all but rather a mystical mingling of so many silvers and pewters that she caught her breath a little at the male beauty of them.

'You've got beautiful eyes,' she heard herself telling him in a soft, slightly slurred... almost sexy voice that she barely recognised as her own.

She was unaware that her own eyes were registering the shock of what she had said as Oliver responded gravely, 'Thank you.'

She was, she recognised, still holding onto her mug, even though his own fingers were now wrapped securely around it—so securely in fact that they were actually touching her own.

Some of that molten silver heat from his eyes must have somehow entered his skin, his blood, she decided dizzily. There could be no other reason for those tiny, darting, fiery sensations of heat that she could feel where her own flesh rested against his.

'So are yours...'

'So are yours'? Uncomprehendingly, Lisa looked at him and watched as he smiled a slow, curling, sensual smile that made her heart soar and turn over and do a bellyflop that left her as shocked and winded as though her whole body had actually fielded a blow.

'Your eyes,' Oliver told her softly. 'Your eyes are beautiful too. Do you always keep them open when you kiss?'

'Why?' Lisa heard herself croak shakily. 'Do you?'

As she spoke her glance was already drifting down to his mouth, as though drawn there by some potent force that she couldn't control.

'That depends,' Oliver was drawling, 'on who I'm kissing...'

He was looking at her mouth now, and a panicky, unfamiliar feeling of mingled excitement and shock kicked into life inside her, bringing with it some much needed sobering sanity, bringing her back to reality.

Lisa gulped and turned her head away, quickly withdrawing her hand from the mug.

'I...I...'

As she fought to find the words to explain away her totally uncharacteristic behaviour and conversation, she was overcome by a sudden fit of sneezing.

Quickly reaching for the box of tissues that Oliver had brought her, she hoped that he would put her flushed complexion down to the fever or the cold that she had obviously caught rather than to her self-conscious embarrassment at what she had said.

What on earth had come over her? She had practically been flirting with him...asking him...inviting him...

Thankfully, Lisa buried her face in another tissue as she sneezed again.

When she had finished, determined to dispel any erroneous ideas that he might have gained from her unguarded and totally foolish comments, she said quickly, 'It must have been wonderful here at Christmas when you were young—your family...this house...'

'Yes, it was,' he agreed, before asking, far too perceptively for Lisa's peace of mind, 'Weren't your childhood Christmases good?'

'Yes, of course they were,' Lisa responded hastily.

'But?' he challenged her.

'My parents travelled a lot with their work. They still do. Whilst I dreamed of traditional Christmases in a house with log fires and a huge tree surrounded by aunts and uncles and cousins, going to church on Christmas morning and doing all the traditional British Christmas things, the reality was normally not roast turkey with all the trimmings but ice cream on an Australian beach or sunshine in Japan.

'My parents did their best, of course. There were always mounds of presents, and they always made sure that we spent Christmas and Boxing Days together, but somehow it just wasn't the same as it would have been if we'd been here... It's silly of me, really, but I suppose a part of me still is that little girl who—'

She stopped, embarrassed by how much of herself she had inadvertently revealed. It must be whatever it was he had obviously added to her hot chocolate that was making her so loquacious and communicative, she thought. She certainly wasn't normally so open or confiding with people she barely knew, although in some odd way it felt as though she had actually known Oliver for a very long time.

She was still frowning over this absurdity when he handed her a glass of amber liquid that he had just poured.

'Drink it,' he told her when she looked at it doubtfully. 'It's pure malt whisky and the best antidote for a heavy cold that I know.'

Reluctantly, Lisa took the glass he handed her. Her head was already swimming slightly, and she felt that the last thing she needed was any more alcohol, but her father was also a great believer in a hot toddy as a cure for colds and so hesitantly she began to sip the tawny golden liquid, closing her eyes as it slid smoothly down her throat, spreading the most delicious sense of beatific warmth throughout her body.

There was something so comforting, so safe, so... so pleasurable about being curled up cosily here in this house...with this man... With this man? What did that mean? Where had that thought come from?

Anxiously Lisa opened her eyes and started to sit up.

'Was that why you wanted to marry Henry, because you thought he could provide you with the traditional lifestyle you felt you'd missed out on?' she heard Oliver asking her.

'Yes...yes, I suppose it was,' she agreed huskily, caught too off guard to think of prevaricating or avoiding the question, and then flushing slightly as she saw the way Oliver was looking at her.

'It would have been a good marriage,' she defended herself. 'We both wanted the same things...' As she saw the way his eyebrows rose, she amended herself shakily, 'Well, I thought that we did.'

'I've heard of some odd reasons for getting married,' she heard Oliver telling her drily, 'but marrying someone because you think he'll provide you with a traditional Christmas has to be the oddest...'

'I wasn't marrying him for that—' Lisa began indignantly, stopping when another volley of sneezing mercifully prevented her from having to make any further response or explanation.

'Come on,' Oliver told her. 'I think it's time you were in bed.'

The whisky that she had drunk was even more potent than she had realised, Lisa acknowledged as Oliver led the way back into the warm, panelled entrance hall and up the stairs.

Just where the stairs started to return towards the galleried landing, Lisa paused to study two large oil paintings hung side by side.

'My grandparents,' Oliver explained, adding informatively, 'My grandfather commissioned the artist to paint them as a first wedding-anniversary present for my grandmother.'

'You look very like him,' Lisa told him. And it was the truth, only the man in the portrait somehow looked less acerbic and much happier than Oliver—much happier and obviously very much in love with his young wife. In the portrait his face was turned slightly towards her matching portrait, so that for a moment it seemed as though the two of them were actually looking at one another.

'It's this way,' Oliver told Lisa, touching her briefly on her arm as he directed her across the landing and towards one of the bedrooms.

'Since my cousin Piers and his girlfriend were supposed to be spending Christmas here a room had already been made up for them and you may as well sleep there.' As he spoke he pushed open one of the seven wooden doors leading off the landing. Lisa blinked dizzily as she stepped inside the room.

It seemed huge—almost as large, she was sure, as the entire floor space of her own small flat. It was so large, in fact, that in addition to the high, king-sized bed there was also a desk and chair and a small two-seater sofa drawn up close to the open fireplace.

'The bathroom's through that door,' Oliver told her, indicating one of a pair of doors set into the wall. 'The other door opens into a walk-in wardrobe.'

A walk-in wardrobe. Lisa blinked owlishly before reminding him, 'Well, that's something I shan't be needing.' When he frowned she explained, 'I don't have any other clothes with me. The others are the ones I—'

'Hurled at me in a fit of temper,' Oliver finished for her.

She had started to shiver again, Lisa noticed, hugging her arms around herself despite the warmth of the bedroom, with its soft fitted carpet and heavy damask curtains.

That whisky really had gone to her head, she acknowledged as a wave of dizziness swept over her, making her sway and reach out instinctively for the nearest solid object to cling onto—the nearest solid object being Oliver himself.

As he detached her hand from his arm she looked up at him muzzily, only to gasp in startled surprise as she was suddenly swung very firmly up into his arms.

'What...what are you doing?' she managed to stammer as he strode towards the bed, carrying her.

'Saving us both a lot of time,' he told her drily as he deposited her with unexpected gentleness on the mattress before asking her, 'Can you manage to get undressed or...?'

'Yes, of course I can,' Lisa responded in a flurry of mingled indignation and flushed self-consciousness, adding defensively, 'I...I just felt a little bit dizzy, that's all...I'm all right now...'

He didn't look totally convinced, and Lisa discovered that she was holding her breath as she watched him walk towards the bedroom door, unable to expel it until she was sure that he had walked through it and closed it behind him.

He really was the most extraordinary man, she decided ten minutes later as she lay in a huge bath of heavenly, deep hot water.

At Henry's parents' house both baths and hot water had been rationed and now it was sheer bliss to ease her aching limbs into the soothing heat, even if something about the steamy atmosphere of the bathroom did somehow seem to increase the dizzying effect that the whisky had had on her system. She felt, she recognised when she eventually reluctantly climbed out of the bath and wrapped herself in one of the huge, warm, fluffy towels on the heated rail, not just physically affected by the alcohol but mentally and emotionally affected by it as well, as though she was on some sort of slightly euphoric high, free of the burden of her normal, cautious, self-imposed restraints.

Shaking her head, she towelled herself dry, remembering only when she had finished that she had no nightclothes.

Shrugging fatalistically, she wrapped herself in another towel instead and padded towards the bed, discarding it as she climbed into the bed's welcoming warmth.

The bedlinen was cotton and deliciously soft against her skin. It smelled faintly of lavender. She breathed in the scent blissfully as she closed her eyes. After the austere regime of Henry's parents' home this was luxury indeed.

She was just on the point of falling asleep when she heard the bedroom door open. In the half-light from the landing she could see Oliver walking towards the bed carrying something.

As he reached the bed she struggled to sit up.

'I've brought you a hot-water bottle,' he told her. 'Just in case you get cold during the night.'

His thoughtfulness surprised her. He was the last person she would have expected to show such consideration, such concern.

Tears filled her eyes as she took it from him, and on some impulse, which when she later tried to rationalise it she could only put down to the effects of the whisky on her system, she reached out and lifted her face towards his, kissing him.

He must have moved, done something . . . turned his head, because she had never intended to kiss him so intimately, only to brush her lips against his cheek in a small gesture of gratitude for his care of her. She had certainly never planned to do anything so bold as kiss him on the lips, but oddly, even though her brain had registered her error, her body seemed to be having trouble responding to its frantic message to remove her mouth from the male one which confusingly, instead of withdrawing from her touch, seemed to be not merely accepting it but actually actively...

Lisa swallowed, panicked, swallowed again and jerked her head back, only to find that somehow or other Oliver's hand was resting on her nape, preventing her from doing anything other than lift her lips a mere breath away from his.

'If that's the way you kissed Henry, I'm not surprised the two of you never went to bed together,' she heard him telling her sardonically. 'If you want to kiss a man you should do it properly,' he added reprovingly, and then before she could explain or even object he had closed the small distance between them and his mouth was back on hers, only this time it wasn't merely resting there against her unintended caress but slowly moving on hers, slowly caressing hers, slowly and then not so slowly arousing her, so that...

It must be the drink, Lisa decided giddily. There could be no other reason why she was virtually clinging to Oliver with both her hands, straining towards him almost as though there was nothing she wanted more than the feel of his mouth against her own.

It *had* to be the drink. There could be no other explanation for the way her lips were parting, positively inviting the masterful male thrust of his tongue. And it had to be the drink as well that was causing her to make those small, keening, soft sounds of pleasure as their tongues meshed.

And then abruptly and shockingly erotically Oliver's mouth hardened on her own, so that it was no longer possible for her to deceive herself that what they were sharing was simply a kiss of polite gratitude. No longer possible at all, especially when the rest of her body was suddenly, urgently waking up to the fact that it actively liked what Oliver was doing and that in fact it would very much like to prolong the sensual, drugging pleasure of the way his mouth was moving on hers and, if at all possible, to feel it moving not just on her mouth but on her...

Shocked by her own reactions, Lisa sobered up enough to push Oliver away, her eyes over-bright and her mouth trembling—not, she admitted inwardly, because he had kissed her, but because he had stopped doing it.

'I never meant that to happen,' she told him huskily, anxious to make sure that he understood that even though she might have responded to him she had not deliberately set out to encourage such intimacy between them.

'I just wanted to say thank you for—'

'For making Henry think you're having an affair with me,' he mocked her as he sat back from her. 'Go to sleep,' he advised her, adding softly, 'unless you want me to take up the invitation these have been offering me...' As he spoke he reached out and very lightly touched one of her exposed breasts.

The bedclothes must have slipped down whilst he'd been kissing her, revealing her body to him, even though she herself hadn't realised it, Lisa recognised. And they hadn't just revealed her body, either, she admitted as her face flushed to a pink as deep as that of her tight, hard nipples.

Quickly she pulled the bedclothes up over herself, clutching them defensively in front of her, her face still flushed, and flushing even deeper as she saw the fleeting but very comprehensive and male glance that Oliver gave her now fully covered body.

'Forget about Henry,' he advised her as he turned to leave. 'You're better off without him.'

He had gone before Lisa could think of anything to say—which in the circumstances was probably just as well, she decided as she settled back into the warmth of the bed. After all, what was there she possibly could have said? Her body grew hot as she remembered the way he had kissed her, her toes curling protestingly as she fought down the memory of her own far from reluctant reaction.

No wonder there had been that male gleam of sensual triumph in his eyes as he'd looked at her body—a look which had told her quite plainly that he enjoyed the knowledge that he had been responsible for that unmistakable sexual arousal of her body—his touch...his kiss...*him*.

It had been an accident, that was all, Lisa reassured herself. A fluke, an unfortunate sequence of events which, of course, would never be repeated. Her toes had relaxed but there was a worrying sensual ache deep within her body—a sense of...of deprivation and yearning which she tried very firmly to ignore as she closed her eyes and told herself sternly to go to sleep.

CHAPTER FIVE

LISA opened her eyes, confused by her unfamiliar surroundings, until the events of the previous evening came rushing back.

Some of those events were quite definitely ones that she did not want to dwell on and which had to be pushed very firmly back where they belonged—in a sealed box marked 'very dangerous'. And some of those events, and in particular the ones involving that unexpectedly passionate kiss she had shared with Oliver, were, quite simply, far too potentially explosive to be touched at all.

Instead she focused on her surroundings, her eyes widening in disbelief as she looked towards the fireplace. She rubbed them and then studied it again. No, they were not deceiving her; there was quite definitely a long woollen stocking hanging from the fireplace—a long woollen stocking bulging with all sorts of odd shapes, with a notice pinned to it reading, 'Open me.'

Her curiosity overcoming her natural caution, Lisa hopped out of bed and hurried towards the fireplace, removed the stocking and then returned to the sanctuary of her bed with it.

As she turned it upside down on the coverlet to dislodge its contents, a huge smile curled her mouth, her eyes dancing with a mixture of almost childlike disbelief and a rather more adult amusement.

Wrapped in coloured tissue-paper, a dozen or more small objects lay on the bed around her. Some of them she could recognise without unwrapping them: the two tangerines, the nuts, the apple...

There could, of course, only be one person who had done this; the identity of her unexpected Father Christmas could not be in doubt, but his motivation was.

Her fingers trembled slightly as she removed the wrapping from what turned out to be a tube of thick white paper. As she unrolled it she began to frown, her frown turning to a soft gasp as she read what had been written on it in impressive copperplate handwriting.

In this year of our Sovereign Queen Elizabeth it is hereby agreed that there shall be a formal truce and a cessation of hostilities between Mistress Lisa and Oliver Esquire in order that the two aforenamed may celebrate the Festival of Christmas in true Christian spirit.

Beneath the space that he had left for her to sign her own name Oliver had signed his.

Lisa couldn't help it. She started to laugh softly, her laugh turning into a husky cough and a fit of sneezes that told her that she had not, as she had first hoped, escaped the heavy cold Oliver had warned likely the previous evening.

At least, though, her head was clear this morning, she told herself severely as she scrabbled around amongst the other packages on the bed, guessing that somewhere amongst them there must be a pen for her to sign their truce.

It touched her to think of Oliver going to so much trouble on her behalf. If only Henry had been half as thoughtful... But Henry would never have done anything like this. Henry would never have kissed her the way Oliver had done last night. Henry would never...

Her fingers started to tremble as she finally found the parcel containing the pen.

It hurt to think that the future that she had believed she and Henry could have together had been nothing more than a chimera ... as childish in its way as her daydreams of a perfect Christmas which she had revealed to Oliver last night, under the effects and influence of his malt whisky.

Her eyes misted slightly with fresh tears, but they were not, this time, caused by the knowledge that she had made a mistake in believing that she and Henry had a good relationship.

After she had signed the truce she noticed that her signature was slightly wobbly and off balance—a reflection of the way she herself had felt ever since Oliver had thrust his way into her life, demanding the return of his cousin's girlfriend's clothes.

Thinking of clothes reminded Lisa that she had nothing to wear other than the things she had discarded the previous evening. Hardly the kind of outfit she had planned to spend Christmas Day in, she acknowledged as she mourned the loss of the simply cut cream wool dress that she had flung at Oliver's feet before her departure from Henry's parents' house.

Still, clothes did not make Christmas, she told herself, and neither did Christmas stockings—but they certainly went a long way to help, she admitted, a rueful smile curling her mouth as she pictured Oliver painstakingly wrapping the small traditional gifts which for generations children had delighted to find waiting for them on Christmas morning.

It was a pity that after such an unexpected and pleasurable start the rest of her Christmas looked so unappealingly bleak. She wasn't looking forward to her return to her empty flat. She glanced at her watch. She had slept much later than usual and it was already nine o'clock—time for her to get up and dressed if she was going to be able to retrieve her car, fill it with petrol and make her return journey to London before dark.

She had just put one foot on the floor when she heard Oliver knocking on the bedroom door. Hastily she put her foot back under the bedclothes and made sure that the latter were secured firmly around her naked body as she called out to Oliver to come in. She didn't want there to be any repeat of last night's still blush-inducing *faux pas* of not realising that her breasts were clearly on view.

The sight of him carrying a tea-tray complete with a china teapot, two cups and a plate of wholemeal toast made her eyes widen slightly.

'So you found it, then. How are you feeling?' he asked her as he placed the tray on the empty half of her bed, half smiling as he saw the clutter of small objects still surrounding her and the evidence of her excitement as she had unwrapped them in the small, shredded pieces of paper torn by her impatient fingers.

'Much better,' Lisa assured him. 'Just as soon as I can get my car sorted out I should be off your hands and on my way back to London. I still haven't thanked you properly for what you did,' she added, half-shyly. Last night the intimacy between them had seemed so natural that she hadn't even questioned it. This morning she was acutely conscious of the fact that he was, after all, a man she barely knew.

His soft, 'Oh, I wouldn't say that,' as he looked directly at her mouth made her flush, but there was more amusement in his eyes than any kind of sexual threat, she acknowledged.

'I haven't thanked you for the stocking either,' she hurried on. 'That was... I... You must think me very childish to want... I'm not used to drinking, and your whisky... I've signed this, by the way.' She tried to excuse herself, diving amongst her spoils to produce the now rerolled truce.

As she did so she suddenly started to sneeze, and had to reach out for the box of tissues beside the bed.

'I thought you said you were feeling all right,' Oliver reminded her sardonically.

'I am,' Lisa defended herself, but now that she was fully awake she had to acknowledge that her throat felt uncomfortably raw and her head ached slightly, whilst yet another volley of sneezes threatened to disprove her claim to good health.

'You're full of a cold,' Oliver corrected her, 'and in no fit state to drive back to London—even if we could arrange for someone to collect your car.'

'But I have to... I must...' Lisa protested.

'Why... in case Henry calls?'

'No,' Lisa denied vehemently, her face flushing again as she suddenly realised how little thought she had actually given to Henry and the end of their romance.

But it was obvious that Oliver had mistaken the cause of her hot face because he gave her an ironic look and told her, 'It will never work. He'll always be tied to his mother's apron strings and you'll always have to take second place to her...

'It's half past nine now,' he told her, changing the subject. 'The village is only ten minutes away by car and we've got time to make it for morning service. I've put the turkey in the oven but it won't be ready until around three...'

Lisa gaped at him.

'But I can't stay here,' she protested.

'Why not?' he asked her calmly. 'What reason have you to go? You've already said that you'll be alone in your flat, and since I'll be alone up here—if you discount a fifteen-pound turkey and enough food to feed the pair of us several times over—it makes sense for you to stay...'

'You want me to stay?' Lisa asked him, astonished. 'But...'

'It will be a hell of a lot easier having you to stay than trying to find a reputable mechanic to sort out and make arrangements for a garage to collect your car, check it over and refuel it. And having one guest instead of two is hardly going to cause me any hardship...' He gave a small shrug.

It was a tempting prospect, Lisa knew. If she was honest with herself she hadn't been looking forward to returning to her empty flat, and even though she and Oliver were virtually strangers there was something about him that... Severely she gave herself a small mental shake.

All right, so maybe last night her body *had* reacted to him in a way that it had certainly never reacted to Henry... Maybe when he had kissed her she *had* felt a certain...need...a response...but that had only been the effect of the whisky...nothing more.

She opened her mouth to decline his invitation, to do the sensible thing and tell him firmly that she had to return home, and instead, to her chagrin, heard herself saying in a small voice, 'Could we really go to church...?' As she realised what she was saying she shook her head, telling him hastily, 'Oh, no, I can't... I haven't anything to wear. My clothes...your cousin's girlfriend's clothes...'

'Are hanging in the closet,' Oliver informed her wryly.

Lisa looked at him. 'What? But they can't be... I left them at Henry's parents'.'

'I didn't,' Oliver informed her succinctly.

'But...but you wanted to give them back to Emma.'

'Originally, yes, but only because Piers was so convinced that the moment she knew what he had done she'd walk out again. However, it transpires that she's off Armani and onto Versace so Piers was allowed to make his peace with her by taking her out and buying her a new wardrobe.'

'So you went to all that trouble for nothing,' Lisa sympathised, knowing how she would have felt in his shoes.

The look he gave her in response made her heart start to beat rather too fast, and for some reason she found it impossible to hold his gaze and had to look quickly away from him.

His slightly hoarse, 'You'd have been wasted on a man like Henry,' made her want to curl her toes in much the same way as his kiss had done last night, and the small shiver that touched her skin had nothing to do with any drop in temperature.

'I'll meet you downstairs in half an hour,' Oliver was saying to her as he moved away from the bed.

Silently, Lisa nodded her agreement. What had she done, committing herself to spend Christmas with him? She gave a small, fatalistic shrug. It was too late to worry about the wisdom of her impulsive decision now.

Thirty-five minutes later, having nervously studied her reflection in the bedroom mirror for a good two minutes, Lisa walked hesitantly onto the landing.

The cream wool dress looked every bit as good on as she had remembered; the cashmere coat would keep her warm in church.

Her hair, freshly washed and dried, shone silkily, and as yet the only physical sign of her cold was a slight pinky tinge to her nose, easily disguised with foundation.

At the head of the stairs she paused, and then determinedly started to descend, coming to an abrupt halt as she reached the turn in the stairs that looked down on the hallway below.

In the middle of the large room, dominating it, stood the largest and most wondrous Christmas tree that Lisa had ever seen.

She gazed at it in rapt awe, unaware that the shine of pleasure in her eyes rivalled that of the myriad decorations fastened to the tree.

As excited as any child, she positively ran down the remaining stairs and into the hall.

'How on earth...?' she began as she stood and marvelled at the tree, shaking her head as she was unable to find the words to convey her feelings.

'I take it you approve,' she heard Oliver saying wryly beside her.

'Yes. Yes. It's wonderful,' she breathed, without taking her eyes off it to turn and look at him. 'But when...how...?'

'Well, I'm afraid I can't claim to have gone out last night and cut it down. It had actually been delivered yesterday. Piers and I were supposed to be putting it up... It's a bit of a family tradition. He and I both used to spend Christmas here as children with our grandparents, and it was our job to "do the tree". It's a tradition we've kept up ever since, although this year...

'I brought it in last night after you'd gone to bed. Mrs Green had already brought the decorations down from the attic, so it was just a matter of hanging them up.'

'Just a matter...' Lisa's eyebrows rose slightly as she studied the rows and rows of tiny lights, the beautiful and, she was nearly sure, very valuable antique baubles combined with much newer but equally attractive modern ones.

'It must have taken you hours,' she objected.

Oliver shrugged.

'Not really.'

'It's beautiful,' she told him, her throat suddenly closing with emotion. He hadn't done it for her, of course. He had already told her that it was a family tradition, something he and his cousin did together. But, even so, to come down and find it there after confiding in him last night how much she longed for a traditional family Christmas...suddenly seemed a good omen for her decision to stay on with him.

'It hasn't got a fairy,' she told him, hoping he wouldn't notice the idiotic emotional thickening in her voice.

As he glanced towards the top of the tree Oliver shook his head and told her, 'Our fairy is a star, and it's normally the responsibility of the woman of the house to put it on the tree, so I left it—'

'You want me to do it?' Fresh emotion swept her. 'But I'm not... I don't belong here,' she reminded him.

'But you are a woman,' he told her softly, and there was something in the way he said the words, something in the way he looked at her that warned Lisa that the kiss they had shared last night wasn't something he had forgotten.

'We'll have to leave it for now, though,' he told her. 'Otherwise we'll be late for church.'

It had been a cold night, and a heavy frost still lay over the countryside, lending it a magical quality of silvered stillness that made Lisa catch her breath in pleasure.

The village, as Oliver had said, was ten minutes' drive away—a collection of small stone houses huddled together on one side of the river and reached by a narrow stone bridge.

The church was at the furthest end of the village and set slightly apart from it, small and weathered and so old that it looked almost as though it had grown out of the craggy landscape around it.

The bells were ringing as Oliver parked the car and then led her towards the narrow lych-gate and along the stone-flagged path through a graveyard so peaceful that there was no sense of pain or sorrow about it.

Just inside the church, the vicar was waiting.

The church was already almost full, but when Lisa would have slipped into one of the rear pews Oliver touched her arm and directed her to one at the front. A family pew, Lisa recognised, half in awe and half in envy.

The service was short and simple, the carols traditional, the crib quite obviously decorated by very young hands, and yet to Lisa the whole experience was more movingly intense than if they had been in one of the world's grandest cathedrals.

Afterwards the vicar was waiting to shake hands and exchange a few words with all his congregation, including them, and as they ambled back to where Oliver had parked the car the final magical seal of wonderment was put on the day when the first flakes of the forecast snow started to fall.

'I don't believe it,' Lisa whispered breathlessly as Oliver unlocked the car doors. 'I just don't believe it.'

As she whirled round, her whole face alight, Oliver laughed. The sound, so spontaneous and warmly masculine, had the oddest effect on Lisa's body. Her heart seemed to flip helplessly, her breathing quickening, her gaze drawn unerringly to Oliver's mouth.

She shouldn't be feeling like this. It wasn't fair and it certainly wasn't sensible. They barely knew one another. Yesterday they had been enemies, and but for an odd quirk of fate they still would be today.

Shakily she walked towards the car, the still falling snowflakes forgotten as she tried to come to terms with what was happening to her.

What exactly *was* happening to her? Something she didn't want to give a name to... Not yet... Perhaps not ever. She shivered as she pulled on her seat belt.

'Cold?' Oliver questioned her, frowning slightly.

Lisa shook her head, refusing to give in to the temptation to look at him, to check and see whether, if she did, she would feel that heart-jolting surge of feminine awareness and arousal that she had just experienced in the car park for a second time.

'Stop thinking about him,' she heard Oliver say harshly to her as she turned away from him and stared out of the window. It took her several seconds to realise that he thought that Henry was the reason for her sudden silence. Perhaps it was just as well he did think that, she decided—for both their sakes.

Through the now drifting heavy snowflakes Lisa could see how quickly they had obscured the previously greeny-brown landscape, transforming it into a winter wonderland of breathtaking Christmas-card white.

Coming on top of the poignant simplicity of a church service which to Lisa, as an outsider, had somehow symbolised all she had always felt was missing from her own Christmases—a sense of community, of sharing... of involvement and belonging, of permanence going from one generation to the next—the sight of the falling snow brought an ache to her throat and the quick silvery shimmer of unexpected tears to her eyes.

Ashamed of her own emotionalism, she ducked her head, searching in her bag for a tissue, hoping to disguise her tears as a symptom of her cold. But Oliver was obviously too astute to be deceived by such a strategy and demanded brusquely, 'What is it? What's wrong?'

adding curtly, 'You're wasting your tears on Henry; he isn't—'

'I'm not crying because of Henry,' Lisa denied. Did he really think that she was so lacking in self-esteem and self-preservation that she couldn't see for herself what a lucky escape she had had, if not from Henry then very definitely from Henry's mother?

'No? Then what are these?' Oliver demanded tauntingly, reaching out before she could stop him to rub the hard pad of his thumb beneath one eye and show her the dampness clinging to his skin. 'Scotch mist?'

'I didn't say I wasn't crying,' Lisa defended herself. 'Just that it wasn't because of... It's not because of Henry...'

'Then why?' Oliver challenged, obviously not believing her.

'Because of this,' Lisa told him simply, gesturing towards the scene outside the car window. 'And the church...'

She could see from the look he was giving her that he didn't really believe her, and because for some reason it had suddenly become very important that he did she took a deep breath and told him quickly, 'It's just so beautiful... The whole thing... the weather, the church service...'

As she felt him looking at her she turned her head to meet his eyes. She shook her head, not wanting to go on, feeling that she had perhaps said too much already, been too openly emotional. Men, in her experience, found it rather discomforting when women expressed their emotions. Henry certainly had.

If Oliver was discomforted by what she had said, though, he certainly wasn't showing it; in fact he wasn't showing any kind of reaction that she could identify at all. He had dropped his eyelids slightly over his eyes and turned his face away from her, ostensibly to concentrate on his driving, making it impossible for her to read his expression at all, his only comment, as he brought the car to a halt outside the house, a cautionary, 'Be careful you don't slip when you get out.'

'Be careful you don't slip...!' Just how old did he think she was? Lisa wondered wryly as she got out of the car, tilting up her face towards the still falling snow-flakes and breathing in the clean, sharp air, a blissful expression on her face as she studied her surroundings, happiness bubbling up inside her.

'I still can't believe this...that it's actually snowing...on Christmas Day... Do you realise that this is my very first white Christmas?' As she whispered the words in awed delight she closed her eyes, took a deep breath of snow-scented air and promptly did what Oliver had warned her not to do and lost her footing.

Her startled cry was arrested almost before it had begun as Oliver reached out and caught hold of her, his strong hands gripping her waist, holding her tightly, safely...

Holding her closely, she recognised as her heart started to pound with unfamiliar excitement and her breath caught in her throat. Not out of shock, Lisa acknowledged, her face flushing as she realised just what it was that was causing her heart and pulse-rate to go into overdrive, and she prayed that Oliver wouldn't be equally quick to recognise that her shallow breathing and sudden tension had nothing to do with the shock of her near fall and everything to do with his proximity.

Why was this happening to her? she wondered dizzily. She didn't even like the man and he certainly didn't like her—even if he *had* offered her a roof over her head for Christmas.

He was standing close enough for her to smell the clean man scent of his skin—or was it just that for some extra-ordinary reason she was acutely sensitive to the scent and heat of him?

Her legs started to tremble—in fact, her whole body was trembling.

'It's all right,' she heard Oliver saying calmly to her. 'I've got you...'

'Yes,' Lisa heard herself responding, her own voice unfamiliarly soft and husky, making the simple affirmation sound something much more sensual and in-viting. Without having had the remotest intention of doing any such thing—it simply wasn't the kind of thing she did—ever—Lisa found that she was looking at Oliver's mouth, and that her gaze, having focused on it for far, far too long, was somehow drawn even more betrayingly to his eyes.

Her breath caught in her throat as she saw the way he was looking back at her, his head already lowering towards hers—as well it might do after the sensually open invitation that she had just given him.

But instead of avoiding what she knew was going to happen, instead of moving away from him, which she could quite easily have done, she simply stood there waiting, with her lips softly parted, her gaze fixed on the downward descent of his head and his mouth, her heart thudding frantically against her chest wall—not in case he kissed her, she acknowledged in semi-shock, but rather in case he didn't.

But of course he did. Slowly and deliberately at first, exploring the shape and feel of her mouth, shifting his weight slightly so that instead of that small but oh, so safe distance between them and the firm grip of his hands on her waist supporting her, it was the equally firm but oh, so much more sensual strength of his body that held her up as his arms closed round her, holding her in an embrace not as intimate as that of a lover but still intimate enough to make her powerfully aware of the fact that he was a man.

Lisa had forgotten that a man's kiss could be like this—slow, thorough and so sensually inventive and promising as he hinted at all the pleasures that there could be to come. And yet it wasn't a kiss of passion or demand—not yet—and Lisa was hazily aware that the slow stroke of his tongue against her lips was more sensually threatening to her self-control than to his, and that she was the one who was having to struggle to pull herself back from the verge of a far more dangerous kind of arousal when he finally lifted his mouth from hers.

'What was that for?' she asked stupidly as she tried to drag her gaze away from his eyes.

'No reason,' he told her in response. But as she started to turn her head away, expecting him to release her, he lifted one hand to her face, cupping the side of her jaw with warm, strong fingers, holding her captive as he told her softly, 'But this is.'

And he was kissing her again, but this time the passion that she had sensed was missing in his first kiss was clearly betrayed in the way his mouth hardened over hers, the way his body hardened against hers, his tongue probing the softness of her mouth as she totally abandoned her normal, cautious behaviour and responded to him with every single one of her aroused senses—every single one.

Her arms, without her knowing quite how it had happened, were wrapped tightly around him, holding him close, her fingertips absorbing the feel of his body, its warmth, its hardness, its sheer maleness; her eyes opened in dazed arousal as she looked up into his, her ears intensely attuned to the sound of his breathing and his heartbeat and their tell-tale quickened rate, the scent of him reaching her with every breath she took, and the taste of him. She closed her eyes and then opened them again as she heard him whispering against her mouth, 'Happy Christmas.'

'Happy Christmas'! Lisa came back to earth with a jolt. Of course. Hot colour flooded her face as she realised just how close she had been to making a complete fool of herself.

He hadn't kissed her because he had wanted her, because he had been overwhelmed by desire for her. He had kissed her because it was Christmas, and if that second kiss had been a good deal more intense than their extremely short-lived acquaintanceship really merited then that was probably her fault for... For what? For responding too intensely to him the first time?

'Happy Christmas!' she managed to respond as she hurriedly stepped back from him and turned towards the house.

As Oliver opened the door for her Lisa could smell the rich scent of the roasting turkey mingling with the fresh crispness of the tree.

'The turkey smells good,' she told him, shakily struggling to appear calm and unaffected by his kiss, sniffing the richly scented air. The kiss that they had so recently exchanged might never have been, judging from the way he was behaving towards her now, and she told herself firmly that it was probably best if she pretended that it hadn't too.

Oliver could never play a permanent role in her life, and this unfamiliar and dangerous intensity of physical desire that she had experienced was something she would be far better off without.

'Yes, I'd better go and check on it,' Oliver agreed.

'I'll come and give you a hand,' Lisa offered, adding as she glanced down at her clothes, 'I'd better go and get changed first, though.'

It didn't take her long to remove her coat and the dress she was wearing underneath it, but instead of re-dressing immediately she found that she was standing staring at her underwear-clad body in the mirror, trying to see it as a man might do... A man? Or Oliver?

Angry with herself, she reached into the wardrobe and pulled out the first thing that came to hand, only realising when she had started to put it on that it was the cream trouser suit which had caused so many problems already.

She paused, wondering whether or not to wear something else, and then heard Oliver rapping on the bedroom door and calling out, 'Lisa, are you all right...?'

'Yes, yes. I'm fine... I'm coming now,' she told him quickly, pulling on the jacket and fastening it. Hardly sensible apparel in which to help cook Christmas lunch, but with the sleeves of the jacket pushed back, she thought... And she could always remove the jacket if necessary. So what if the pretty little waistcoat that went underneath it was rather brief? Oliver was hardly likely to notice, was he?

He was waiting for her outside the bedroom door, and caught her off guard by catching hold of her arm and placing his hand on her forehead.

'Mmm... no temperature. Well, that's something, I suppose. Your pulse is very fast, though,' he observed as his hand circled her wrist and he measured her pulse-rate.

Quickly Lisa snatched her wrist away. 'I've just got a cold, that's all,' she told him huskily.

'Just a cold,' he reiterated. 'No broken heart...'

Lisa flashed him a doubtful look, half suspecting him of deliberately mocking her, but unable to make any response, knowing that she would be lying to him if she tried to pretend that she felt anything other than half-ashamed relief at breaking up with Henry.

'You might not want to accept it now, but you didn't really love him,' Oliver told her coolly. 'If you had—'

'You have no right to say that,' Lisa objected suddenly, angry with him—and, more tellingly, with herself, without wanting to analyse or really know why.

'What do you know about love?'

'I know enough about it to recognise it when I see it—and when I don't,' Oliver countered as she fell silent, but Lisa wasn't really listening; she was too caught up in the shock of realising that the pain spearing her, pinning her in helpless, emotional agony where she stood, was caused by the realisation that for all she knew there could have been, could still be a woman in Oliver's life whom he loved.

'Stop thinking about it,' she heard Oliver telling her grimly, her face flushing at the thought that he had so easily read her mind and guessed what she was feeling, until he added, 'You must have seen for yourself that it would never have worked. Henry's mother would never have allowed him to marry you.'

Relief made her expel her breath in a leaky sigh. It had been Henry whom he had warned her to stop thinking about and not him. He had not guessed what she had been thinking or feeling after all.

'I thought we'd agreed a truce,' she reminded him, adding softly, 'I still haven't thanked you properly for everything you've done. Helping—'

'Everything?'

For some reason the way he was looking at her made her feel closer to the shy teenager she had once been than the adult woman she now was.

'I meant...' she began, and then shook her head, knowing that she wouldn't be able to list all the reasons she had to thank him without at some point having to look at him, and knowing that once she did her gaze would be drawn irresistibly to his mouth, and once it was...

'I... That turkey smells wonderful.' She gave in cravenly. 'How long did you say it would be before we could eat?'

She could tell from the wry look he gave her as she glanced his way that he wasn't deceived, but to her relief he didn't push matters, leaving her to follow him instead as he turned back towards the stairs.

CHAPTER SIX

'I NEVER imagined you'd be so domesticated.'

They were both in the large, well-equipped, comfortable kitchen, Lisa mixing the ingredients for the bread sauce whilst Oliver deftly prepared the vegetables, and she knew almost as soon as she had voiced her surprise that it had been the wrong thing to say. But it was too late to recall her impulsive comment because Oliver had stopped what he was doing to look frowningly across at her.

'I'm sorry,' she apologised ruefully. 'I didn't mean to—'

'To sound patronising,' Oliver supplied for her.

Lisa glanced warily at him and then defended herself robustly, telling him, 'Well, when we first met you just didn't seem the type to—'

'The "type".' Oliver pulled her up a second time. 'And what "type" would that be, exactly?'

Oh, dear. He had every right to sound annoyed, Lisa acknowledged.

'I didn't mean it the way it sounded,' she confessed. 'It's just that Henry—'

'Doesn't so much as know how to boil an egg,' Oliver supplied contemptuously for her. 'And that's something to be admired in a man, is it?'

Lisa's face gave her away even before she had protested truthfully, 'No, of course it isn't.'

'The reason Henry chooses to see even the most basically necessary domestic chores such as cooking for himself as beneath his male dignity is because that's the way his mother has brought him up and that's the way she intends him to stay. And woe betide any woman who doesn't spoonfeed her little boy the way she's taught him to expect.'

There was no mistaking the disgust in Oliver's voice as he underlined the weakness of Henry's character and Lisa knew that there was no real argument that she could put forward in Henry's defence, even if she had wanted to do so.

'It might come as something of a surprise to you,' Oliver continued sardonically, obviously determined to drive home his point, 'but, quite frankly, the majority of the male sex—at least the more emotionally mature section of it—would not take too kindly at having Henry held up to them as a yardstick of what it means to be a man. And neither, for future reference, do most of us relish being classified as a "type".'

'I didn't mean it like that,' Lisa protested. 'It's just that when we first met you seemed so... I could never have imagined you...us...' She was floundering, and badly, she recognised, adding lamely, 'I wasn't comparing you to Henry at all.'

'No?' Oliver challenged her.

'No,' Lisa insisted, not entirely truthfully. She *had* been comparing them, of course, but not, as Oliver fortunately had incorrectly assumed, to his disadvantage. Far from it... She certainly didn't want to have to explain to him that there was something about *him* that was so very male that it made laughable the idea that he should in any way fail to measure up to Henry.

Measure up to him! When it came to exhibiting that certain quality that spelled quite essential maleness there was simply no contest between them. Oliver possessed it, and in abundance, or so it seemed to Lisa, and Henry did not have it at all. She was faintly shocked that she should so clearly recognise this—and not just recognise it, she admitted uneasily. She was quite definitely somehow or other very sensitively aware of it as a woman—too aware of it for her peace of mind.

'I happen to have an orderly mind,' Oliver was telling her, thankfully unaware of what she was thinking, 'and I loathe any unnecessary waste of time. To live in the midst of chaos and disorder seems to be totally counter-productive, and besides...' he gave a small shrug and drained the peeled and washed potatoes, turning away from her as he started to cut them, so that she could not see his expression '...after my mother died and my father and I were on our own, we both had to learn how to look after ourselves.'

Lisa discovered that there was a very large lump in her throat as she pictured the solemn, lonely little boy and his equally lonely father struggling together to master their chores as well as their loss.

'The behavioural habits one learns as a child have a tendency to become deeply ingrained, hence my advice to you that you are well rid of Henry. He will never cease being his mother's spoilt and emotionally im-mature little boy...' His tasks finished, he turned round and looked directly at her as he added drily, 'And I suspect that you will never cease thinking of Christmas as a specially magical time of year...'

'No, I don't expect I shall,' Lisa admitted, adding honestly, 'But then I don't really want to. I don't suppose I'll ever stop wanting, either, to put down roots, to marry and have children and to give them the stability and per-manence I missed as a child,' she confessed, wanting to be as open and honest with him as he had been with her.

'I know a lot of my friends think that I'm rather odd for putting more emphasis on stability and the kind of relationship that focuses more on that than on the romantic and sexual aspects of love—'

'Does there have to be a choice?' Oliver asked her.

Lisa frowned. 'What do you mean?'

'Isn't it possible for there to be romance and good sex between a couple, as well as stability and permanence? I thought the modern woman was determined to have it all. Emotional love, orgasmic sex, a passionately loyal mate, children, career...'

'In theory, yes,' Lisa agreed ruefully. 'But I suppose if I'm honest...I'm perhaps not very highly sexed. So—'

'Who told you that? Henry?'

'No,' she said, stung by the mocking amusement that she could see in his eyes, aware that she had allowed herself to be drawn onto potentially very treacherous ground and that sex was the very last topic she should be discussing with this particular man—especially when her body was suddenly and very dangerously reinforcing the lack of wisdom in her laying claim to a low libido when it was strongly refuting that. Too strongly for her peace of mind. Much, much too strongly.

'I...I've always known it,' she told him hastily, more to convince herself, she suspected, than him.

'Always...?' The way the dark eyebrows rose reminded her of the way he had looked when he had come round to see her and demand the return of Emma's clothes, and that same frisson of danger that she had felt then returned, but this time for a very, very different reason.

'Well, from when I was old enough... When I knew... After...' she began, compelled by the look he was giving her to make some kind of response.

'You mean you convinced yourself that you had a low sex drive because, presumably, that was what your first lover told you,' Oliver challenged her, cutting through her unsuccessful attempts to appear breezily nonchalant about the whole thing.

'It wasn't just because of that,' Lisa defended herself quickly and, she realised uneasily, very betrayingly.

'No?' Oliver's eyebrows rose again. 'I'll take a bet that there haven't been very many... Two, maybe three at the most, and that, of course, excludes Henry, who—'

'Three...?' Lisa was aghast. 'Certainly not,' she denied vehemently. 'I would never...' Too late she realised what she was doing... what she was saying.

It was one thing for her to feel that, despite the amusement of her peers, she had the sort of nature that would not allow her to feel comfortable about sharing the intimacy of her body with a variety of lovers and that her low sex drive made it feel right that there had only been that one not really too successful experience in her late teens, and it was one thing to feel that she could quite happily remain celibate and wait to re-explore her sexuality until she found a man she felt comfortable enough with to do so, but it was quite another to admit it to someone like Oliver, who, she was pretty sure, would think her views archaic and ridiculous.

'So, there has only been one.' He pounced, immediately and humiliatingly correct. 'Well, for your information, a man who tells a virgin that she's got a low sex drive tends to be doing so to protect his own inadequacy, not hers.'

Her inadequacy! Lisa drew in a sharp breath of panic at the fact that he should dare so accurately and acutely to put her deepest and most intimate secret fears into words, and promptly fought back.

'I'm twenty-four now, not eighteen, and I think I know myself well enough to be able to judge for myself what kind of sex drive I have...'

'You're certainly old enough and, I would suspect, strong-willed enough to tell yourself what kind of sex drive you think it safe to allow yourself to have,' Oliver agreed, staggering her with not just his forthrightness but his incisive astuteness as well.

Pride warred with caution as Lisa was torn between demanding to know exactly what he meant and, more cravenly, avoiding what she suspected could be a highly dangerous confrontation—highly dangerous to her, that was. Oliver, she thought, would thoroughly enjoy dissecting her emotional vulnerabilities and laying them out one by one in front of her.

In the end caution won and, keeping her back to him, she told him wildly, 'I think this bread sauce is just about ready... What else would you like me to do?'

She thought she heard him mutter under his breath, 'Don't tempt me,' before he said far more clearly, 'Since it's Christmas Day I suppose we should really eat in the dining room, although normally I prefer to eat in here. I'll show you where everything is, and if you could sort it all out—silver, crystal, china...'

'Yes... of course,' Lisa agreed hurriedly, finding a cloth to wipe her hands on as she followed him back into the hall.

The dining room was a well-proportioned, warm, panelled room at the rear of the house, comfortably large enough to take a table which, Oliver explained to her, could be extended to seat twelve people.

'It was a wedding present to my grandparents. In those days, of course, twelve was not a particularly large number. My grandmother was one of seven and my grandfather one of five.'

'Oh, it must be wonderful to be part of a large family,' Lisa could not help commenting enviously. 'My parents were both onlys and they only had me.'

'Being an only child does have its advantages,' Oliver told her firmly. 'I'm an only myself, and—'

'But you had the family—aunts, uncles, cousins...'

'Yes,' Oliver agreed.

But he had also lost his mother at a very vulnerable age, Lisa recognised, and to lose someone so close must inevitably have a far more traumatic effect on one's life than the mere absence of a non-existent extended family.

'I can guess what you're thinking,' she told him wryly. 'I just sound pathetically self-absorbed and self-pitying. I know how much both my parents need their work, their art, how important it is to them. It's just that...'

'There have been times when you needed to know that you came first,' Oliver guessed shrewdly. 'There are times when we all feel like that,' he told her. 'When we all need to know that we come first, that we are the most important person in someone else's life... What's wrong?' he asked when he saw the rueful acknowledgement of his perception in Lisa's eyes.

'Nothing,' she said. 'It's just that I can't... that you don't...' She shook her head. 'You seem so self-contained,' was the only thing she could say.

'Do I?' He gave her a wry look. 'Maybe I am now. It wasn't always that way, though. The reason for the breakup of my first teenage romance was that my girl-friend found me too emotionally demanding. She was right as well.'

'You must have loved her an awful lot,' was all she could find to say as she tried to absorb and conceal the unwanted and betraying searing surge of envy that hit her as she listened to him.

'I certainly thought I did,' Oliver agreed drily, 'but the reality was little more than a very intense teenage crush. Still, at least I learned something from the experience.'

What had she been like, the girl Oliver had loved as a teenager? Lisa wondered ten minutes later when he had returned to the kitchen and she was removing silverware and crystal from the cupboards he had shown her.

She found it hard to imagine anyone—*any* woman—rejecting a man like him.

Her hand trembled slightly as she placed one of the heavy crystal wineglasses on the table.

What was the matter with her? she scolded herself. Just because he had kissed her, that didn't mean... It didn't mean anything, and why should she want it to? If she was going to think about any member of the male sex right now she ought to be thinking about Henry. After all, less than twenty-four hours ago she had believed that she was going to marry him.

It unnerved her a little bit to realise how far she had travelled emotionally in such a short space of time. It was hard to imagine now how she could ever have thought that she and Henry were suited—in any way.

'I really don't think I should be drinking any more of this,' Lisa told Oliver solemnly as she raised the glass of rich red wine that he had just refilled to her lips.

They had finished eating fifteen minutes earlier, and at Oliver's insistence Lisa was now curled up cosily in one corner of the deep, comfortable sofa that he had drawn up close to the fire and where she had been ordered to remain whilst he stacked the dishwasher.

The meal had been as good as any Christmas dinner she could ever remember eating and better than most.

It had amazed her how easily the conversation had flowed between them, and what had surprised her even more was to discover that he was a very witty raconteur who could make her laugh.

Henry had never made her laugh.

Hastily she took a quick gulp of her wine. It was warm and full-bodied and the perfect accompaniment for the meal they had just enjoyed.

When they had left the table to come and sit down in front of the fire to finish their wine, Oliver had closed the curtains, and now, possessed by a sudden urge to see if it was still snowing, Lisa abandoned her comfortable seat and walked rather unsteadily towards the curtained window.

The wine had been even stronger than she had believed, she admitted. She wasn't drunk—far from it— but she certainly felt rather light-headed and a little giddy.

As she tugged back the curtain she gave a small, soft sigh of delight as she stared through the window.

It was still snowing—thick, whirling-dervish-like, thick white flakes, like those in a child's glass snowstorm. As she looked up into the darkening sky she could see the early evening stars and the thin sickle shape of the moon.

It was her childhood dream of a white Christmas come true. And to think that if she had returned to London as she had originally planned to do she would have missed it! Emotion caught her by the throat.

She dropped the curtain, turning back into the room, stopping as she saw Oliver watching her. She hadn't heard him come back in and unaccountably she could feel herself starting to tremble slightly.

'What is it? What's wrong?' he asked her.

'Nothing,' she denied. 'It's just...' She gave a small shrug, closed her eyes and then opened them again as the darkness increased the heady effects of the wine. 'It's just that all of this...is so...so perfect,' she told him huskily, gesturing to the room and then towards the window and the view that lay beyond it. 'So...so magical... This house...the weather...the tree...church this morning...my stocking and...'

'And...?' Oliver prompted softly.

He was looking at her very intently—so intently, in fact, that she felt as though she could drown in the dark intensity of his eyes, as though she was being compelled to...

'And you,' she breathed, and as she said it she felt her heart slam fiercely against her chest wall, depriving her of breath, whilst the silence between them seemed to pulse and quicken and to take on a life of its own.

'I really shouldn't drink any more of this,' she heard herself whispering dizzily as she picked up her glass and took a nervous gulp, and then watched as Oliver walked softly towards her.

'No, you really shouldn't,' he agreed as he reached her and took the glass from her unresisting fingers, and then he took her equally unresisting body in his arms and her quiescent mouth into the warm captivity of his.

'We shouldn't be doing this,' she reproached him, mumbling the words against his mouth, her arms wrapped around him, her fingers burrowing into the thick darkness of his hair, her eyes luminous with the desire that was turning her whole body into molten liquid as she gazed up into his eyes.

'Oh, yes, we should,' was his sensuously whispered response. 'Oh, yes, we most definitely, assuredly should.' And then he was kissing her again. Not forcefully, but oh, so compellingly that it was impossible for her to resist him—impossible for her to want to resist him.

'You've already kissed me once for Christmas,' Lisa reminded him unsteadily as he slowly lifted his mouth from hers and looked down at her.

'This isn't for Christmas,' he whispered back as his hand slid under her hair, tilting her head back up towards him, sliding his other hand down her back, urging her closer to his own body.

Lisa could feel her heart hammering against her ribs as sensations that she had never experienced before—not with Henry and certainly not with the man who had been her first and only lover—flooded her body.

'Then what is it for?' she forced herself to ask him huskily.

'What do you think?' Oliver responded rawly. 'I wanted you the first time I saw you—did you know that?'

'How could you have done?' Lisa argued. 'You were so furious with me, and—'

'And even more furious with myself... with my body for the way it was reacting to you,' Oliver told her, adding rawly, 'The same way it's reacting to you right now.'

Uncertainly Lisa searched his face. Everything was happening so quickly that she couldn't fully take it all in. If she had felt dizzy before, with the combination of the rich wine and the warm fire, that was nothing to the headiness affecting her now, clouding her ability to reason logically, making her heart thump dangerously, heavily as her body reacted to what was happening to her—to them.

'I'll stop if you want me to,' she heard Oliver telling her hoarsely as he bent his head and gently nuzzled the soft, warm flesh of her throat. As she stifled the small, betraying sound she made when her body shuddered in shocked pleasure Lisa shook her head.

'No. No. I don't want you to stop,' she admitted huskily.

'Good,' Oliver told her thickly. 'Because I don't want to either. What I want is you, Lisa... God, how I want you.'

'I'm not used to this,' Lisa said shakily. 'I don't—'

'Do you think that I am... that I do?' he interrupted her almost roughly. 'For God's sake, Lisa, have you any idea how long it is since I was this intimate with a woman... since I wanted to be this intimate with a woman? I'm not a teenager,' he half growled at her when she shook her head. 'I don't normally... It's been a hell of a long time since anyone has affected me the way you do... One hell of a long time.'

Lisa was trembling as he took her back in his arms, but not because she was afraid. Oh, no, not because of anything like that.

At any other time the eagerness with which she met Oliver's kiss would have shocked her, caused her to deny what she was experiencing, but now, for some reason, things were different—*he* was different. This was Christmas, after all—a special, magical time when special, magical things could happen.

As she felt the probing thrust of Oliver's tongue she reached out towards him, wrapping her arms around him, opening her mouth to him.

Somewhere outside this magical, firelit, pine-scented world where it seemed the most natural thing of all for her and Oliver to come together like this there existed another, different world. Lisa knew that, but right now... right now...

As she heard the rough deep sound of pleasure that Oliver made in his throat when he tasted the honeyed interior of her mouth Lisa gave up trying to think and behave logically. There was no point and, even more important, there was no need.

Instead, as she slid her fingers through the thick softness of Oliver's hair, she let her tongue meet his—slowly, hesitantly at first, such intimacy unfamiliar to her. The memories of her much younger, uncertain teenage explorations recalled sensations which bore no resemblance whatsoever to the sensations she was experiencing now as Oliver's tongue caressed hers, the weight of his body erotically masculine against the more slender femininity of her own as his hands caressed her back, her waist, before sliding down over her hips to cup the soft swell of her buttocks as he lifted her against him.

Lisa knew already that he was aroused, but until she felt the taut fullness of his erection against her own body she hadn't realised how physically and emotionally vulnerable and responsive she was to him. A sensation, a need that was totally outside her previous experience overtook her as she felt the liquid heat filling her own body, her hips lifting automatically, blindly seeking the sensual intimacy that her flesh craved.

'So much for your low sex drive,' she heard Oliver muttering thickly against her ear, before he added throatily, 'You're one hell of a sexy lady, Lisa. Do you know that? Do you know what you're doing to me...? How you're making me feel...? How you've made me feel since you stood there in your flat in that damned suit, with your breasts...?'

Lisa heard him groan as his hand reached upwards towards her breast, sliding beneath the fabric that covered it to cup its soft, eager weight, his thumb-tip caressing the hard peak of her nipple.

'Let me take this off,' he urged her, his hands removing her jacket, and then starting on the buttons of the waistcoat underneath it, his eyes dark with arousal as he looked deeply into hers. And then, without waiting for her to respond, his mouth curled in a small, sensual half-smile and he bent his head and kissed her briefly but very hard on her half-parted mouth. 'I want to see you, Lisa—all of you. I want to touch you, hold you, taste you, and I want you to want to do the same as me.'

Lisa knew that he must have felt the racking, sensual shudder that convulsed her body even if he hadn't heard her immediate response to the mental image that his words had aroused, in the low groan she was not quite able to suppress.

'You want that,' he pressed huskily. 'You want me to undress for you. You want to see me...to touch me...' He was kissing her again now—slow, lingering kisses all over her face and throat—whilst his hands moved deftly, freeing her from her clothes. But it wasn't the thought of her own nakedness beneath his hands that was causing her breath to quicken and her heart to lurch frantically against her ribs, but rather the thought of his nakedness beneath hers.

What was happening to her? she wondered dazedly. Her, to whom the thought of a man's naked body was something which she normally found rather discomforting and not in the least erotic. What was happening that she should now be so filled with desire that her whole body ached and pulsed with it at the mere thought of seeing Oliver's? The mere thought... Heaven knew what she would be like when that thought became a reality, when she was free to reach out and touch and taste him too.

Helplessly she closed her eyes, and then opened them again to find Oliver watching her.

'*Is* that what you want, Lisa?' he asked her softly whilst his thumb-tip drew a sensual line of pleasure around her sensitised mouth. 'Is that what you want— to see me...touch me...feel me...?'

Dry-mouthed, Lisa nodded. Her top was unfastened now, and she was vaguely aware of the half-exposed curves of her breasts gilded by the firelight, but her own semi-nudity seemed unimportant and irrelevant; her whole concentration was focused on Oliver, on the deft, steady movements of his hands as he unfastened the buttons on his shirt, his gaze never wavering from her as he started to remove it.

His chest was broad and sleekly muscled, tanned, with a dark arrowing of silky black hair down the centre, the sight of which made her muscles clench and her breath leak from her lungs in a rusty ache of sensory overload. His nipples, flat and dark, looked so different from her own.

As his hands reached for the fastening on his trousers, Lisa leaned forward, acting on impulse. The scent of him filled her nostrils, clouding her thought processes, drugging her...

As her lips closed around the small dark nub of flesh, she made a soft sound of feminine pleasure deep in her throat. Her tongue-tip circled his flesh, stroked it, explored the shape and texture of it before she finally returned to sucking gently on it.

'Lisa.'

The shock of being wrenched away from him was like having her whole body plunged in icy-cold water after it had been lapped in tropical warmth, the pain so great that it made her physically ache and cry out, her shocked gaze focusing in bewilderment on Oliver's, quick emotional tears filming her eyes as she wondered what it was she had done, why it was that he was being so cruelly brutal with her.

'It's too much, too soon,' she heard him telling her harshly. 'I can't... It's...'

Still half in shock she watched him as he shook his head.

'You're turning me on too much,' he told her more gently, 'and I can't...'

Lisa could feel the shock of it all the way through her body—the shock and an intensely feminine thrill that she could have such a powerful effect on him. As though he had guessed what she was feeling, she heard Oliver groan softly, and then he was reaching for her, holding her in his arms before she could evade them, kissing her now tightly closed eyelids, and then her mouth, and then he was telling her, 'Another few seconds of that and right now I'd be inside you and without—' He broke off and then added, 'That isn't how I want it to be for our first time together.'

Lisa moved instinctively against him, and then tensed as she felt the rough brush of his body hair against her naked breasts.

As she bent her head to look down at where her top had slid away from her Oliver's gaze followed hers, and then he bent his head, slowly easing her top completely away from her as he gradually kissed his way down her body, stopping only when he had reached the dark pink tautness of her nipple.

As he closed his mouth on it, repeating on her the caress she had given him, Lisa tensed in shock beneath the surge of pleasure that arced through her, arching her spine, locking her hands against his head, making her shudder as her body, beneath the weight of the flooding waves of pleasure that pulsed through her, was activated by the now urgent suckle of his mouth on her breast.

Was this how *he* had felt when she had caressed him in the same way? No, it couldn't have been, she denied. She could feel what he was doing to her, right deep down within her body, her womb. She could feel... With a small, shocked gasp she started to push him away.

'What is it?' she heard Oliver asking thickly as he released her nipple. He was breathing heavily and she could feel the warmth against her skin resensitising it, making her...

'I...' Nothing, she had been about to respond, but instead she heard herself saying helplessly in an unfamiliar and huskily sensual voice, 'I want you, Oliver... I want you.'

'Not one half as much as I want you,' he responded tautly as she quickly removed the remainder of her clothes and his own, and then, like a mystical, almost myth-like personification of all that was male inspired by some Greek legend, and filling her receptive senses with that maleness, he knelt over her, his dark head bowed as he gently eased her back against the soft fabric of the sofa and made love to her with a sensuality that took her breath away.

It didn't matter that no man had ever touched her, caressed her, kissed her so intimately before or that she had never imagined wanting one to do so. Somehow, when it was Oliver's hands, Oliver's mouth that caressed her...

So this was desire, need, physically wanting someone with an intensity that could scarcely be borne.

Lisa gasped, caught her breath, held out her arms, her body opening to him, wanting him, enfolding him as she felt the first powerful thrust of him within her and then felt it again and again until her whole world, her whole being was concentrated on the powerful, rhythmic surge of his body within her own and the sensation that lay beyond it—the ache, the urgency... the release...

Lisa heard herself cry out, felt the quickening thrust of Oliver's body, the hard, harsh sound of his breathing and his thudding heartbeat as she clung to him, moved with him, against him, aching, urging and finally losing herself completely, drowning in the liquid pulse of pleasure that flooded through her.

Later, still drowsy, sated, relaxed as she lay within the protective curve of Oliver's body, she told him sleepily, 'I think this is the best Christmas I have ever had.'

She could feel as well as hear him laughing.

'You do wonders for my ego, do you know that?' he told her as he tilted her face up to his own and kissed her lingeringly on the mouth.

'It's the truth,' Lisa insisted, her eyes clouding slightly as she added more self-consciously, 'I... I never realised before that it could be so... That I could feel...'

'It?' Oliver teased her.

'Sex,' Lisa told him with dignity.

'Sex?' She heard the question in his voice. She looked uncertainly up at him. He looked slightly withdrawn, his expression stern, forbidding... more like the Oliver she had first met than the man who had just held her in his arms and made such wonderful, cataclysmic, orgasmic love to her.

'What's wrong?' she asked him hesitantly, her heart starting to thump nervously. Wasn't this what all the books warned you about—the man's withdrawal and coldness after the act of sex had been completed, his desire to separate himself from his partner whilst she wanted to maintain their intimacy and to share with him her emotional awe at the physical pleasure their bodies had given one another?

'What we just shared may have been sex to you,' he told her quietly, 'but for me it was more than that. For me it was making love in the true sense of those words.

Experimenting teenagers, shallow adults without maturity or sensitivity have sex, Lisa...'

'I don't understand,' she told him huskily, groping through the confusion of her thoughts and feelings to find the right words. 'I... You... We don't really know one another and...'

'And what?' Oliver challenged her. 'Because of that we can't have any feelings for one another?' He shook his head. 'I disagree.'

'But until today...until now...we didn't even like one another... We...'

'We what?' Oliver prompted her as she came to an uncertain stop. 'We were very physically aware of one another.'

Lisa opened her mouth to deny what he was saying and then closed it again.

'Not so very long ago you told me that you wanted me,' Oliver reminded her softly, 'and I certainly wanted you. I agree that the circumstances under which we met initially clouded our ability to judge one another clearly, but fate has given us an opportunity to start again...a second chance.'

'Twenty-four hours ago I was still planning to marry Henry,' Lisa protested helplessly.

'Twenty-four hours ago I still wanted to wring your pretty little neck,' Oliver offered with a smile.

'What's happening to us, Oliver?' she asked him uneasily. 'I don't understand.' She sat up and pushed the heavy weight of her hair off her face, her forehead creased in an anxious frown. 'I just don't do things like this. I've never... I thought it must be the wine at first... That...'

'That what? That the effect of three glasses of red wine was enough to make you want me?' He gave her a wry look. 'Well, I haven't even got that excuse. Not then, and certainly not now,' he added huskily as he reached towards her and took hold of her hand, guiding it towards his body whilst he bent his head and kissed her slowly.

To be aroused by him the first time might just possibly have been some kind of fluke, Lisa acknowledged, but there was no way she could blame her desire for him now on the wine. Not a second time, not now. And she did desire him, she acknowledged shakily as her fingers explored the hard strength of him. Oh, yes, she did want him.

It was gone midnight before they finally went upstairs, Lisa pausing to draw back the curtains and look out on the silent, snow-covered garden.

'It's still snowing,' she whispered to Oliver.

'Mmm...' he agreed, nuzzling the back of her neck. 'So it is... Lovely...'

But it wasn't the view through the window he was studying as he murmured his rich approval, and Lisa laughed softly as she saw the way he was studying her still naked breasts.

'No,' Oliver said to her, shaking his head as she paused outside the guest-bedroom door. 'Tonight I want you to sleep with me...in my bed...in my arms,' he told her, and as she listened to him Lisa felt her heart flood with emotion.

It was too soon yet to know just how she really felt about him, or so she told herself. And too dangerous, surely, when her body was still flooded with the pleasure he had given it? She was by nature cautious and careful; she always had been. It wasn't possible for her to fall in love over the space of a few hours with a man she barely knew.

But then less than twenty-four hours ago she would also have vehemently denied that it was possible for her to want that same man so much and with such a degree of intensity that, as he drew her towards his bed and held out his arms to her, her body was already starting to go liquid with pleasure and yearning for him.

CHAPTER SEVEN

'OUCH. That's not fair. I was retying the snowman's scarf.'

Lisa laughed as Oliver removed from his collar the wet snow of the snowball she had just thrown at him, quickly darting out of the way as he bent down mock-threateningly to make a retaliatory snowball of his own.

She had been awoken two hours earlier by the soft thud of a snowball against the bedroom window, Oliver's half of the bed that they had shared all night being empty. Intrigued and amused, she had slid out of bed, wrapping the quilt around her naked body as she'd hurried across to the window. As she'd peered out she'd been able to see beneath the window Oliver standing in the garden next to a huge snowman, a pile of snowballs stacked at his feet.

'At last, sleepyhead, I thought you were never going to wake up,' he'd teased her as she had opened the window, laughing at her as she'd gasped a little at the cold shock of the frosty air.

'I'm not sleepy,' Lisa had corrected him indignantly. 'It's just that I'm...' she had begun, and then had stopped, flushing slightly as she'd acknowledged the real reason why her body was aching so deliciously, why her energy so depleted.

As Oliver had looked silently back at her she had known that he too was remembering just why it was that she had fallen into such a deep sleep in the early hours of the morning.

116

She was remembering the night, the *hours* they had spent together again now as she went to help him brush the snow from his collar, the scent of him, overlaid by the crisp, fresh smell of the snow, completely familiar to her now and yet at the same time still headily erotic.

When previously she had read of women being aroused by the body smell of their lover she had wrinkled her own nose just a little fastidiously, never imagining that there would ever come a time when she not only knew just how those women had felt but also actively wanted— no, *needed,* she corrected herself as her stomach muscles clenched on a weakening surge of emotion—to bury her face against her lover's body and breathe his scent, to trace the outline of his bones, his muscles, absorb the texture of his flesh and the whole living, breathing essence of him.

'It's too soon for this ... for us ...' she had whispered shakily last night in the aftermath of their second loving. 'We can't be ...'

'Falling in love,' Oliver had supplied for her, and had challenged her softly between kisses. 'Why not? People do.

'What is it you're really afraid of, Lisa?' he had asked her later still, after his mouth had caressed every inch of her body, driven her to unimaginable heights of ecstasy and he had whispered to her that she was everything he had ever dreamed of finding in a woman...everything he'd begun to think he would never find, and she had tensed in his arms, suddenly afraid to let herself respond to him as her senses were urging her to do, to throw caution to the wind to tell him what she was feeling.

'I'm afraid of this,' she had whispered huskily back, 'of you ...'

'Of me?' He held her slightly away from him, frowning at her in the darkness. 'Look, I know the circumstances surrounding our initial meeting weren't exactly auspicious, and yes, I agree, I did rather come the heavy, but to be confronted with Piers within thirty minutes of my plane landing from New York after a delay of over five hours and to discover what he'd done—'

'No, it's not that,' Lisa assured him quickly. She was fully aware now that the arrogance that she had believed she had seen in him was simply part of a protective mask behind which he hid his real personality. 'It's us...us together,' she told him, searching for the right words to express her feelings. 'I'm afraid that...everything's happening so fast. And it's not...I'm not...

'This isn't how I ever thought it would be for me,' she told him simply in the end. 'I never imagined I could feel so...that I could...' She paused, fumbling for the words and blushed a little as she tried to tell him how bemused, how shocked, almost, she still was by the intensity not just of his desire for her but of her own for him. It was so out of character for her, she told him, so unexpected...

'So unwanted,' he guessed shrewdly.

'It isn't how I thought my life was going to be,' she persisted. 'None of it seems quite real, and I'm afraid. I don't know if I can sustain this level of emotional intensity, Oliver... I feel like a child who has been handed a Christmas gift so far outside its expectations that it daren't believe it's actually got it. I'm afraid of letting myself believe because I'm afraid of the pain I'll suffer if...if it proves not to be real after all.'

'Don't you think I feel exactly the same way?' Oliver challenged her.

'You've been in love before,' she told him quietly. 'You've experienced this kind of sexual intimacy... sexual ecstasy before, but I—'

'No.' He shook his head decisively. 'Yes, I'm more sexually experienced than you are, but *this*... Take my word for it, Lisa—this is something different... something special.

'Look,' he added when she said nothing. 'With all this snow, there's no way either of us can leave here now until it thaws; let's use the time to be together, to get to know one another, to give our feelings for one another a chance. Let's suspend reality, if you like, for a few days and just allow ourselves to feel instead of questioning, doubting...'

He had made it all sound so easy, and it was easy, Lisa acknowledged now as his arms closed around her. Too easy... That was the trouble.

Already after only a few short, fateful hours she was finding it hard to imagine how she had ever lived without him and even harder to imagine how she could ever live without him in the future. It would be so easy simply to close her eyes, close her mind to her thoughts and concentrate instead on her feelings. She could feel her heart starting to thump heavily with the intensity of her emotions.

'Stop worrying,' Oliver whispered against her mouth, correctly guessing what she was thinking. 'Everything's going to be fine. We're going to be fine.'

'This really is the best Christmas I have ever had,' she told him huskily ten minutes later as he lifted his mouth from hers.

'*You* are the best Christmas I have ever had,' Oliver responded. 'The best Christmas I ever will have.'

* * *

In the end they had four full days together, held for three of them in a captivity from which neither of them truly wanted to escape by the icy frost that kept the roads snowbound. And during those four days Lisa quickly discovered how wrong she had been in her original assessment of Oliver as being arrogantly uncaring.

He did care, and very deeply, about those who were closest to him but, as he freely admitted, the loss of his mother whilst he had still been so young had made him cautious about allowing others to get too close to him too quickly.

'But of course there are exceptions to every rule,' he had told her huskily, 'and *you* are my exception.'

She had given up protesting then that it was too soon for them to be in love. What was the point in denying what she knew she felt about him?

'I still can't believe that this... that we... that it's all really happening,' she whispered to Oliver on the fourth morning, when the thaw finally set in, her voice low and hushed, as though she was half-afraid of even putting her doubts into words.

'It *is* happening,' Oliver reassured her firmly, 'and it's going to go on happening for the rest of our lives.'

They were outside, Lisa watching as Oliver chopped logs to replace those they had used. Dressed in jeans and a black T-shirt, he had already discarded the checked woollen shirt that he had originally been wearing, the muscles and tendons on his upper arms revealed by the upward swing of the axe as he chopped the thick fir trunks into neatly quartered logs.

There was something about watching a man engaged in this kind of hard physical activity that created a feminine frisson of awareness of his masculinity, Lisa acknowledged as Oliver paused to wipe the sweat from his skin. She didn't want this special time that they were sharing to come to an end, she admitted. She was afraid of what might happen when it did. Everything had happened so fast—too fast?

'Nearly finished,' Oliver told her, mistaking the reason for her silence. 'I should be back from New York by the end of the week,' he added as Lisa bent down to retrieve the logs that he had already cut and carry them over to where the others were neatly stacked.

Lisa already knew that he was booked on a flight to New York to complete some protracted and difficult business talks he had begun before Christmas—the reason he had been so irritable and uncompromising the first time they had met, he had explained to her.

'I wish I didn't have to go,' he added, 'but at least we'll be able to spend New Year's Eve together and then... When are your parents due back from Japan?'

'Not until the end of February,' Lisa told him.

'That long.' He put down the axe and demanded hastily, 'Come here.'

Automatically Lisa walked towards him. The hand he extended to cup the side of her face and caress her skin smelled of freshly cut wood and felt slightly and very, very sensually abrasive, and the small shiver that ran through her body as he touched her had nothing to do with being cold.

'I could take some leave at the end of January and we could fly out to Japan together to see them then...'

Lisa knew what he was suggesting and her heart gave a fierce bound. So far they had not talked seriously about the future. Oliver had attempted to do so but on each occasion she had forestalled him, not wanting to do or say anything that might destroy the magic of what they were sharing, fearing that by allowing reality and practicality into their fragile, self-created world they might damage it. Their relationship, their love was so different from anything she had ever imagined experiencing or wanting to experience that part of her was still half-afraid to trust it... half of her?

And besides, she had already written to her parents to tell them that she and Henry would be getting engaged at Christmas and, whilst she suspected that they would never have been particularly keen on the idea of having Henry for a son-in-law, she felt acutely self-conscious about suddenly informing them that she had fallen head over heels in love with someone else.

It was so out of character for her, and the mere thought of having to confess her feelings for Oliver to anyone else made her feel defensive and vulnerable. She had always taken such a pride in being sensible and level-headed, in making carefully thought-out and structured decisions about her life. She wasn't sure how she herself really felt about this new aspect to her personality yet, never mind being ready to expose it to anyone else.

'What's wrong?' Oliver asked her as he felt her tensing against his touch. 'You don't seem very happy with the idea of me meeting your parents.'

'It's not that,' Lisa denied. There was, she had discovered, an unexpected corner of vulnerability in him which she suspected sprang from the loss of his mother— something that, if not exactly a fear of losing those close to him, certainly made him slightly more masculinely possessive than she would have expected in such an otherwise controlled and strongly emotionally grounded man. And it was, at least in part, because of this vulnerability that she had felt unable to tell him of her own fears and uncertainties.

'No? Then what exactly is it? Or is that yet another subject you don't want to discuss?' Oliver asked her sarcastically as he released her and picked up the axe, hefting it, raising it and then bringing it down on the log that he had just positioned with a force that betrayed his pent-up feelings.

Dismayed, Lisa watched him. What could she say? How could she explain without angering him still further? How could she explain to him what she felt when she truthfully didn't fully understand those feelings herself?

'It isn't that I don't want you to meet them,' she insisted. 'It's just ... well, they don't even know yet that Henry and I aren't ...' She knew immediately that she had said the wrong thing and winced as she witnessed the fury with which Oliver sliced into the unresisting wood, splitting it with one unbelievably powerful blow, the muscles in his arms cording and bunching as he tightened his grip on the axe.

'You're saying that they'd prefer you to be marrying Henry, is that it?' he suggested dangerously.

'No, of course they wouldn't,' Lisa denied impatiently. 'And besides, I'm old enough to be able to make up my own mind about who I want to commit myself to.'

'Now we're coming to it, aren't we?' Oliver told her, throwing down the axe and confronting her angrily, his hands on his hips, the faded fabric of his jeans stretching tautly against his thighs.

Just the sight of him made her body ache, Lisa acknowledged, but physical desire, sexual desire, could surely never be enough to build an enduring relationship on? And certainly it was not what she had envisaged building a lifetime's commitment on.

'It's not your parents who might reject me, is it, Lisa? It's you... Despite everything that has happened, all that we've shared.'

'No, that isn't true,' Lisa denied.

'Isn't it?' Oliver bit out grimly as he turned away from her to pick up another large chunk of wood.

Numbly Lisa watched him manhandling it onto the trestles that he was using to support the fir trunks whilst he chopped them into more easily manageable pieces. Above them the sky had started to cloud over, obliterating the bright promise of the morning's sunshine, making her feel shivery and inadequately protected from the nasty, raw little wind which had sprung up, even in the fine wool jacket she was wearing.

The weather, she recognised miserably, was very much only echoing what was happening to them—the bright promise of what they had shared was being threatened by the ominous thunderclouds furrowing Oliver's forehead and her own fear that what he had claimed he felt for her might prove too ephemeral to last.

After all, wasn't the classic advice always to treat falling in love too quickly and too passionately with caution and suspicion? Wasn't it an accepted rationale that good love—real love—needed time to grow and didn't just happen overnight?

As she watched Oliver silently releasing his anger on the wood, his jaw hardening a little bit more with each fierce blow of the axe, Lisa knew that she couldn't blame him for what he was feeling, but surely he could understand that it wasn't easy for her either? She was not programmed mentally for the kind of thing that had happened to her with him; she had not been prepared for it either, not...

'There's no need for you to stay.'

Lisa stared at Oliver as she heard the harsh words, the cutting edge to his voice reminding her more of the man she had first met than the lover she had become familiar with over the last few precious days.

'The wind's getting cold and you're shivering,' he added when she continued to stare mutely at him. 'You might as well go back inside; I've nearly finished anyway.'

He meant that there was no need for her to stay outside and wait for him, Lisa realised, and not that she might as well leave him and start her return journey home, as she had first imagined.

The relief that filled her was only temporary, though. Didn't the fact that she had so easily made such a mistake merely confirm what her sense of caution was already trying to make her understand—that she didn't really *know* Oliver, that no matter how compatible they might be in bed out of it there were still some very large and very important gaps in their knowledge of each other?

Quietly she turned away from him and started to walk back towards the house. Behind her she heard the sound of the axe hitting a fresh piece of wood. She had almost reached the house when she heard Oliver calling her name. Stopping, she turned to watch him warily as he came running towards her.

As he reached her he took hold of her, wrapping her in his arms, telling her fiercely, 'God, Lisa, I'm such a... I'm sorry... the last thing I want us to do is fight, especially when we've got so little time left... Lisa?'

As she looked up at him he cupped her face in his hands, his thumbs caressing her skin, his hair tousled from the wind, his eyes dark with emotion.

Standing close to him like this, feeling the fierce beat of his heart and the heat of his body, breathing in the scent of him, unable to resist the temptation to lift her hand and rub away the streak of dried earth on his cheek, to feel already the beginning of the growth of his beard on his jaw which he had shaved only that morning, Lisa acknowledged that she might just as well have downed a double helping of some fatally irresistible aphrodisiac.

'Lisa...'

His voice was lower now, huskier, more questioning, and she knew that the shudder she could feel going through him had nothing to do with the after-effects of the punishing force he had used to cut up the logs.

She was the one who was responsible for that weakness, for that look in his eyes, that hardness in his body, and she knew that she was responding to it, as unable to deny him as he was her, her body nestling closer to his, her head lifting, her lips parting as he started to kiss her, tenderly at first and then with increasing passion.

'I can't bear the thought of losing you,' he whispered to her minutes later, his voice husky and raw with emotion. 'But you don't seem so concerned. What is it, Lisa...? Why won't—?'

'It's too soon, Oliver, too early,' Lisa protested, interrupting him, knowing that if she didn't stand her ground now, if she allowed her brain to be swayed not just by his emotions.but by her own as well, it would be oh, so fatally easy, standing with him like this now, held in his arms, to believe that nothing but this mattered—it would be too late, and there would be no one but herself to blame if at some future date she discovered...

'I could make you commit yourself to me,' Oliver warned her, his mood changing as his earlier impatience returned. 'I could take you to bed now and show you...'

'Yes, you could,' Lisa agreed painfully. 'But can't you see, Oliver...? Please try to understand,' she begged him. 'It isn't that I don't love you or want you; it's just that...this...this...us...isn't how I envisaged it would be for me. You're just not the kind of man I—'

'You mean that I'm not Henry,' Oliver supplied harshly for her, his arms dropping back to his sides as he stepped back from her.

Lisa closed her eyes. Here we go again, she thought tiredly. She had meant one thing and Oliver had taken the words to mean something completely different—just as she had misunderstood him earlier when she had thought he was telling her to leave. And if they could misunderstand one another so easily what real chance did they have of developing the harmonious, placid relationship that she had always believed she needed? Some people enjoyed quarrels, fights, emotional highs and lows, but she just was not one of them.

'I don't want to fight with you, Oliver,' she told him quietly now. 'You must know that you have no possible reason to feel...to think that I want you to be Henry...'

'Haven't I?' he demanded bitterly. 'Why not? After all, you were prepared to marry him. Wanted to marry him... Wanted to so much in fact that you were prepared to let his mother browbeat and bully you and—'

'That's not true,' Lisa interrupted him swiftly. 'Look, Oliver, please,' she protested, spreading her hands in a gesture of emotive pleading for his temperance and understanding. 'Please... I can't talk. I don't want us to argue...not now, when everything has been so...perfect, so special and—'

'So perfect and special in fact that you don't want to continue it,' Oliver cut across her bitterly.

'You've given me the most wonderful Christmas I've ever had,' she whispered huskily, 'in so many different ways, in all the best of ways. Please don't spoil that for me...for us...now. I need time, though, Oliver; we *both* need time. It's just...'

'Just what?' he demanded, his eyes still ominously watchful and hard. 'Just that you're still not quite sure...that a part of you still thinks that perhaps Henry—?'

'No. Never,' Lisa insisted fiercely, adding more emotionally, 'That's a horrible thing to say. Do you really think that if I had any doubts about...about wanting you, that I would have—?'

'I didn't say that you don't prefer me in bed,' Oliver told her curtly, correctly guessing what she had been about to say, 'but the implication was there none the less—in the very words you used to describe what you wanted from marriage the first time we discussed it, the fact that you've been so reluctant to accept what's happening between us...the fact that you don't seem to want me to meet your parents.'

'You've got it all wrong,' she protested. 'My feelings...my doubts,' she amended when he snorted derisively over her use of the word 'feelings', 'they...they don't have anything to do with you. It isn't because I don't...because I don't care; in fact—'

'Oh, no,' Oliver told her cynically, not allowing her to finish what she was saying.

'It's me...not you,' Lisa told him. 'I've always been so cautious, so...so sensible... This...this falling in love with you—well, it's just so out of character for me and I'm afraid.'

'You're afraid of what?' he demanded.

The wind had picked up and was flattening his T-shirt against his body, but, unlike her, he seemed impervious to the cold and Lisa had to resist the temptation to creep closer to him and beg him to wrap his arms protectively around her to hold her and warm her.

'I don't know,' she answered, lifting her eyes to meet his as she added, 'I'm just afraid.'

How could she tell him without adding to his anger that a good part of what she feared was that he might fall out of love with her as quickly as he had fallen in love with her? He was quite obviously in no mood to

understand her vulnerability and fear and she knew that
he would take her comment as an indication that she
did not fully trust him, an excuse or a refusal to commit
herself to him completely.

'Please don't let's quarrel,' she repeated, reaching out
her hand to touch his arm. His skin felt warm, the
muscles taut beneath her touch, and the sensation of his
flesh beneath her own even in this lightest of touches
overwhelmed her with such an intense wave of desire
that she had to bite down hard on her bottom lip to
prevent herself crying out her need to him.

They were still standing outside, and through the
windows she could see the tree that he had decorated for
her, the magic he had created for her.

'Oh, Oliver,' she whispered shakily.

'Let's go inside,' he responded gruffly. 'You're getting
cold and I'm... You're right,' he added rawly. 'We
shouldn't be spoiling what little time we've got left.'

'It is still Christmas, isn't it?' Lisa asked him semi-
pleadingly as he turned to open the door for her.

'Yes, it's still Christmas,' he agreed, but there was a
look in his eyes that made her heart ache and warned
her that Christmas could not be made to last for ever—
like their love?

Was *that* why she doubted it—him? Because it seemed
too perfect, too wonderful...too precious to be real?

They said their private goodbyes very early in the
morning in the bedroom they had shared for the last
four nights, and for Lisa the desolation which swept over
her at the thought that for the next two nights to come
she would not be sleeping within the protection of his
arms, next to the warmth and intimacy of his body, only
confirmed what in her heart of hearts she already knew.

It was already too late for her to protest that it was too soon for them to fall in love, too late to cling to the sensible guidelines that she had laid down for herself to live her life by—the sensible, cautious, pain-free guidelines which in reality had been submerged and obliterated days ago—from the first time that Oliver had kissed her, if she was honest—and there were tears in her eyes as she clung to him and kissed him.

What was she doing? she asked herself helplessly. What did guidelines, common sense, caution or even potential future heartache matter when they had this, when they had one another; when by simply opening her mouth and speaking honestly and from her heart she could tell Oliver what she was feeling and that she had changed her mind, that the last thing she wanted was to be apart from him?

'Oliver...' she began huskily.

But he shook his head and placed his fingertips over her mouth and told her softly, 'It's all right—I know. And I do understand. You're quite right—we do need time apart to think things through clearly. I've been guilty of trying to bully you, to coerce you into committing yourself to me too soon. Love—real love—doesn't disappear or vanish when two people aren't physically together; if anything, it strengthens and grows.

'I didn't mean to put pressure on you, Lisa, to rush you. We both have lives, commitments, career responsibilities to deal with. The weather has given us a special opportunity to be together, to discover one another, but the snow, like Christmas, can't last for ever.

'If I'd managed to get you to come to New York with me as I wanted, I probably wouldn't have got a stroke of work done,' he told her wryly. 'And a successful conclusion to these negotiations is vitally important for the future of the business—not just for me personally but for everyone else who is involved in it as well. Oh, and by the way, don't worry about not taking your car now; I'll make arrangements to have it picked up and returned to you later. I don't want you driving with the roads like this.'

Oliver had already told her about a large American corporation's desire to buy out part of his business, leaving him free to concentrate on the aspects of it he preferred and giving him the option to work from home.

'If Piers goes ahead and marries Emma, as he's planning, he's going to need the security of knowing he has a good financial future ahead of him. Naturally the Americans want to get the business as cheaply as they can.' He had started to frown slightly, and Lisa guessed that his thoughts were not so much on her and their relationship but on the heavy responsibility that lay ahead of him.

Her throat ached with pain; she desperately wanted to reach out to him and be taken in his arms, to tell him that she had made a mistake, that she didn't want to let him go even for a few short days. But how could she now after what he had said?

Suddenly, illuminatingly, she realised that what she had feared was not loving him but losing him. The space that she had told herself she needed—they both needed—had simply been a trick her brain had played on her, a coping mechanism to help her deal with the pain of being without his love.

Quietly she bowed her head. 'Thank you,' Lisa whispered to him as tears blurred her eyes.

'Are you sure there's nothing else you want...a book or...?'

Lisa shook her head. 'You've already bought me all these magazines,' she reminded Oliver huskily, indicating the pile of glossies that he had insisted on buying for her when they'd reached the station and which he was still carrying for her, together with her case, as he walked her along the platform to where the train was waiting.

She had tried to protest when he had insisted on buying her a first-class ticket but he had refused to listen, shaking his head and telling her, 'That damned independence of yours. Can't you at least let me do something for you, even if it's only to ensure that you travel home in some degree of comfort?'

She had, of course, given in then. How could she not have done so? How could she have refused not just his generosity but, she sensed, from the expression in his eyes at least, his desire to protect and cherish her as well?

'Make sure you have something to eat,' he urged her as they reached the train. 'It will be a long journey and...'

And she wouldn't be spending it eating, Lisa thought as he went on talking. Nor would she be doing anything more than flipping through the expensive magazines he had bought her. No, what she would be doing would be trying to hold back the tears and wishing that she were with him, thinking about him, reliving every single moment they had spent together...

A family—mother, father, three small children— paused to turn round and hug the grandparents; the smallest of them, a fair-haired little boy, clung to his grandmother, telling her, 'I don't want to go, Nana... Why can't you come home with us...?'

'I have to stay here and look after Grandpa,' his grandmother told him, but Lisa could hear the emotion in her voice and see the tears she was trying not to let him see.

Why did loving someone always seem to have to cause so much pain?

'Oh, to be his age and young enough to show what you're feeling,' Oliver murmured under his breath.

'It wouldn't make any difference if I did beg you to come home with me,' Lisa pointed out, trying to sound light-hearted but horribly aware that he must be able to hear the emotion in her voice. 'You'd still have to go to New York. We'd still have to be apart...'

'Yes, but I... At least I'd know that you want me.'

It was too much. What was the point in being sensible and listening to the voice of caution when all she really wanted to do was to be with him, to be held in his arms, to tell him that she loved and wanted him and that all she wanted—all she would ever want or need—was to be loved by him?

He was looking at her... watching... waiting almost.

'Oliver...' She wanted so desperately to tell him how she felt, to hear him tell her that he understood her vulnerability and that he understood all the things she hadn't been able to bring herself to say, but the guard was already starting to close the carriage doors, advancing towards them, asking her frowningly, 'Are you travelling, miss, because if so...?'

'Yes... Yes...'

'You'd better get on,' Oliver advised her.

She didn't want to go. She didn't want to leave him. Lisa could feel herself starting to panic, wanting to cling to him, wanting him to hold her... reassure her, but he was already starting to move away from her, lifting her case onto the train for her, bending his head to kiss her fiercely but far, far too briefly.

She had no alternative. She had to go.

Numbly Lisa stepped up into the train. The guard slammed the door. She let down the window but the train was already starting to move.

'Oliver. Oliver, I love you...'

Had he heard her, or had the train already moved too far away? She could still see him…watching her…just.

Oliver waited until the train had completely disappeared before turning to leave, even though Lisa had long since gone from view. If only he didn't have these damned negotiations to conclude in New York. He wanted to be with Lisa, wanted to find a way to convince her.

Of what…? That she loved him?

Lisa pushed open the door of her flat and removed the pile of mail which had accumulated behind it. Despite the central heating, the flat felt cold and empty, but then that was perhaps because *she* felt cold and empty, Lisa recognised wryly—cold without Oliver's warmth beside her and empty without him…his love.

In her sitting room the invitation she had received from her friend Alison before Christmas to her annual New Year's Eve party was still propped up on the mantelpiece, reminding her that she would have to ring Alison and cancel her acceptance. The telephone started to ring, breaking into the silence. Her heart thumping, she picked up the receiver.

'You got home safely, then.'

'Oliver.'

Suddenly she was smiling. Suddenly the world was a warmer, brighter, happier place.

'Lisa, I've been thinking about what you said about us not rushing into things…about taking our time…'

Something about the sombreness in his voice checked the happiness bubbling up inside her, turning the warmth at hearing his voice to icy foreboding.

'Oliver…'

Lisa wanted to tell him how much she was missing him, how much she loved him, but suddenly she wasn't sure if that was what he wanted to hear.

'Look, Lisa, I've got to go. They've just made the last call for my flight...' The phone line went dead.

Silently she replaced the receiver. Had it really only been this morning that he had held her in his arms and told her how much he loved her? Suddenly, frighteningly, it was hard to believe that that was true. It seemed like another world, another lifetime, already in the past... over... as ephemeral as the fleeting magic of Christmas itself.

'No... it's not true,' she whispered painfully under her breath. 'He loves me; he said so.' But somehow her reassurance lacked conviction.

Even though she had been the one to insist that it was too soon for them to make a public commitment to one another, that they both needed time, she wished passionately now that Oliver had overruled her, that he had confirmed the power and strength of his love for her. How? By refusing to let her leave him?

What was the matter with her? Lisa asked herself impatiently. Could she really be so illogical, saying one thing, wanting another, torn between her emotions and her intelligence, unable to harmonise the two, keeping them in separate compartments in much the same way as Oliver had accused her of doing with sex and marriage?

Had she after all any real right to feel chagrined at the sense of urgency, almost of impatience in his voice as he had ended his brief call? She had, she admitted, during the last few days grown accustomed to being the sole focus of his attention, and now, when it was plain that he had something else on his mind...

She frowned, aware that instead of feeling relief when he had told her that he agreed that they did need time to think things over she had actually felt—*still* felt—hurt and afraid, abandoned, vulnerably aware that he might be having second thoughts about his feelings for her.

How ironic if he had—especially since she had spent almost the entire journey home dwelling on the intensity of her own feelings and allowing herself to believe...

It would only be a few days before they were together again, she reminded herself firmly. Oliver had promised that he would be back for the New Year and that they would spend it together. There would be plenty of time for them to talk, for her to tell him how much she loved and missed him.

Even so... Sternly she made herself pick up her case and carry it through to her bedroom to unpack. A small, tender smile curled her mouth as she picked up the stocking that she had so carefully packed—the stocking that Oliver had left for her to find on Christmas morning.

There were other sentimental mementoes as well—a small box full of pine needles off the tree, still carrying its rich scent, the baubles that Oliver had removed from it and hung teasingly on her ears one night after dinner, a cracker that they had pulled together... She touched each and every one of them gently.

Through what he had done for her to make her Christmas so special Oliver had revealed a tender, compassionate, emotional side to his nature that made it impossible for her not to love him, not to respond to the love he had shown her. *Had* shown her?

Stop it, she warned herself. Stop creating problems that don't exist. Determinedly, she started to unpack the rest of her things.

CHAPTER EIGHT

IT WAS New Year's Eve and almost three o'clock in the
afternoon, and still Oliver hadn't rung. Lisa glared at
the silent telephone, mentally willing it to ring. She had
been awake since six o'clock in the morning and
gradually, as the hours had ticked by, her elation and
excitement had changed to edgy apprehension.

Where *was* Oliver? *Why* hadn't he been in touch? Was
he just going to arrive at her door without any warning
so that he could surprise her, instead of telephoning be-
forehand as she had anticipated?

Nervously she smoothed down the skirt of her dress
and just managed to restrain herself from checking her
reflection in the mirror for the umpteenth time.

She had spent most of her free time the previous day
cleaning the flat and shopping for tonight. The lilies she
had bought with such excitement and pleasure were now
beginning to overpower her slightly with their scent. The
champagne waiting in the fridge was surely chilled to
perfection; the special meal she had cooked last night
now only required reheating. Oliver might be planning
to take her out somewhere for dinner, but the last thing
she wanted was to have to share him with anyone else.

And even if she had dressed elegantly enough to dine
at the most exclusive restaurant in town and her hair was
immaculately shiny, her make-up subtly enhancing her
features, it was not to win the approval of the public at
large that she had taken such pains with her appearance,
or donned the sheer, silky stockings, or bought that out-

rageously expensive and far too frothily impractical new silk underwear. Oh, no!

Where *was* Oliver? Why hadn't he been in touch? The small dining table which was all her flat could accommodate was lovingly polished and set with her small collection of good silver and crystal—unlike Oliver's grandparents she did not possess a matching set of a dozen of anything, and her parents—peripatetic gypsy souls that they were—would have laughed at the very idea of burdening themselves with such possessions.

However, through her work Lisa had developed a very good eye for a bargain, and the small pieces that she had lovingly collected over the years betrayed, she knew, the side of her nature that secretly would have enjoyed nothing better than using her dormant housewifely talents to garner a good old-fashioned bridal bottom drawer.

To help pass the time she tried to imagine Oliver's eventual arrival, her heartbeat starting to pick up and then race as she visualised herself opening the door to him and seeing him standing there, reaching out for her, holding her, telling her how much he had missed her and loved her.

Oliver, where are you? Where are you...?

Almost on cue the telephone started to ring—so much on cue in fact that for several seconds Lisa could only stand and listen to the shrill sound of it, before realising that she wasn't merely imagining it and that it had actually rung, was actually ringing.

A little to her own disgust she realised as she picked up the receiver that her hand was actually trembling slightly.

'Lisa...'

Her heart sank.

'Oliver...where are you? When will you—?'

'Bad news, I'm afraid.' Oliver cut her off abruptly. 'I'm not going to be able to make it after all; I'm stuck in New York and—'

'What?'

There was no way Lisa could conceal her feelings—shock, disappointment, almost disbelief, and even anger was sharpening her voice as she tried to take in what he was telling her. A horrid feeling of sick misery and despair was beginning to fill her but Lisa's pride wouldn't let her give in to it, although her hand was clenched so tightly on the receiver that her skin was sharp white over her knuckles.

'I'm still in New York,' she heard Oliver telling her, his voice curt and almost—so her sensitive ears told her—hostile as he added brusquely, 'I know it's not what I'd planned but there's simply nothing I can do...'

Nothing he could do or nothing he *wanted* to do?

All the doubts, the fears, the insecurities and the regrets that Lisa had been holding at bay ever since they had had to part suddenly began to multiply overwhelming and virtually obliterating all her self-confidence, her belief in Oliver's love. She had been right to be mistrustful of his assurances, his promises; she had been right to be wary of a love that had sprung into being so easily and now, it seemed, could just as easily disappear.

'Lisa?' Oliver said sharply.

'Yes, I'm still here.'

It was an effort to keep her voice level, not to give in to the temptation to beg and plead for some words of reassurance and love, but somehow she managed to stop herself from doing so, even though the effort made her jaw ache and her muscles lock in painful tension.

'You do understand, don't you?' he was asking her.

Oh, yes, she understood. How she understood.

'Yes,' she agreed indistinctly, her voice chilly and distant as she tried to focus on salvaging her pride instead of giving in to her pain. 'I understand perfectly.'

She wasn't going to weaken and let herself ask when he would be coming home, or why he had changed his mind...so obviously changed his mind.

Before he could say any more and before, more importantly, she could break down and reveal how hurt and let down she was feeling, Lisa fibbed tersely, 'I must go; there's someone at the door.' And without waiting to hear any more she replaced the receiver. She must not cry, she *would* not cry, she warned herself fiercely.

In the mirror she caught sight of her reflection; her face was paper-white, her eyes huge, revealing all too clearly what she was feeling, the contrast between her carefully made-up face and the misery in her eyes somehow almost pathetically grotesque.

Her flat, her clothes, her whole person, she decided angrily, made her feel like some modern-day Miss Havisham, decked out all ready for the embrace of a man who had deserted her. The thought was unbearable. She couldn't stay here, not now...not when everything around her reminded her of just how stupid she had been. Why, even now she was still emotionally trying to find excuses for Oliver, to convince herself that she had overreacted and that he felt as bad as she did and that he wasn't having second thoughts.

Alison's invitation was still on her mantelpiece. She reached for the telephone.

'Of course you can still come, you didn't need to ask,' Alison reproved her when she'd explained briefly that there had been a change in her plans and that she was now free for the evening. 'What happened? Has Henry—?'

'It's all off with Henry,' Lisa interrupted her.

There hadn't been time to explain to Alison just what had happened when she had telephoned her to ask her how her skiing holiday had gone and cancel her acceptance to her party and now Lisa was grateful for this omission, even though it did give her a small twinge of guilt when Alison immediately and staunchly, like the good friend she was, declared, 'He's let you down, has he? Well, you know my feelings about him, Lisa. I never thought he was the right man for you. Look, why don't you come over now? Quite a few people are coming early to help but we can always use another pair of hands.'

'Oh, Alison...'

Ridiculously, after the way she had managed to control herself when she'd been speaking to Oliver, she could feel her eyes starting to fill with tears at her friend's sturdy kindness.

'Forget him.' Alison advised her. 'He's not worth it...he never was. You may not believe me now, but, I promise you, you are better off without him, Lisa. Now go and put your glad rags on and get yourself over here... Are we going to party!'

As she replaced the telephone receiver Lisa told herself that Alison's words applied just as much to Oliver as they did to Henry, although for very different reasons.

Forget him. Yes, that was what she must do.

Tonight, with the old year ending and the new one beginning, she must find a way of beginning it without Oliver at her side. Without him in her life.

On impulse she went into the kitchen and removed the champagne from the fridge, pouring herself a glass and quickly drinking it. It was just as well that Alison's flat was within reasonably easy walking distance, she decided as the fizzy alcohol hit her empty, emotionally tensed stomach.

There was no need for her to get changed; the little black dress she was wearing—had put on for Oliver— was very suitable for a New Year's Eve celebration. All she had to do was redo her make-up to remove those tell-tale signs of her tears.

She poured herself a second glass of champagne, re- alising too late that instead of filling the original glass, which still had some liquid in the bottom, she had ac- tually filled the empty one—Oliver's glass. Grimacing slightly, she picked them both up and carried them through to her bedroom with her, drinking from one before placing them both on the table beside her bed and then quickly repairing her make-up.

In New York Piers frowned as he walked into his cousin's hotel suite and saw Oliver seated in a chair, staring at the telephone.

'Is something wrong?' he asked him. His curiosity had been alerted earlier by the fact that Oliver had been ex- tremely impatient to bring their discussions with the Americans to a conclusion, stating that he had to return to England without explaining why. Piers had happened to be looking at him when they had heard the news that the talks would have to continue. Oliver had been none too pleased.

'No,' Oliver responded shortly. Why had Lisa been so distant with him—so uninterested, so curt to the point of dismissal? She had every right to be angry and even upset about the fact that he had had to change their plans, but she had actually sounded as though she hadn't wanted to see him.

'Well, Jack Hywell is anxious to get on with the nego- tiations,' Piers told him. 'Apparently he's due to take his kids away the day after tomorrow, which is why he wants to take the discussion through the New Year period.

'Oh, by the way, Emma rang me this morning. She's been up to Yorkshire, and whilst she was up there she heard that Henry is getting married. Apparently, he's marrying someone he's known for a while. I must admit I'm surprised his mother finally sanctioned a marriage. Still, good luck to him, I say, and to her.

'What is it?' he asked Oliver. 'Hey, Oliver, watch it...' he warned his cousin as he watched the latter's hand clench tightly on the glass he was holding. 'Look, I know how much pressure these negotiations are putting you under,' he commiserated, 'but with any luck they'll be over soon now, and... Oliver, where are you going?'

'Home,' Oliver told him brusquely.

'Home? But you *can't*,' Piers protested. 'The negotiations.'

Oliver snarled at him, telling him in no uncertain terms what should be done with the negotiations and leaving the room.

Piers stared open-mouthed at his departing back. Oliver hardly ever swore, and he certainly never used the kind of language that Piers had just heard him use. He was normally so laid back... Something was obviously wrong, but what?

'Ugh?'

Reluctantly Lisa opened her eyes. What *was* that noise? Was someone really banging a hammer inside her head or was someone at the door?

Someone was at the door. Flinging back the duvet, she reached for her robe, wincing at both the pain in her aching head and the state of her bedroom—clothes scattered everywhere in mute evidence of the decidedly unsober state in which she had returned to her flat in the early hours of the morning. She had never had a strong head for alcohol, she admitted to herself, and Alison's punch had been lethal. She would have to ring her later and thank her for the party, and for everything else as well.

'Don't even think about it,' Alison had advised Lisa drolly the previous evening after she had determinedly rescued her from the very earnest young man who had buttonholed her.

'He's even worse than Henry,' she had warned Lisa, rolling her eyes. 'He still lives with his parents and his hobby is collecting beetles or something equally repulsive. I only invited him because it was the only way I could escape from his mother. I know how much you like a lame dog, but really, Lisa, there are limits. Has he invited you round to look at his beetle collection yet?' she asked wickedly, making Lisa laugh in spite of herself.

'That's better,' she had approved, adding more seriously, 'I hadn't realised that Henry meant quite so much to you, but—'

'It isn't Henry,' Lisa had started to say, but someone had come up and dragged Alison away before she could explain properly and after that, rather than cause her friend any more concern, she had forced herself to be more enthusiastic and convivial, the result of which was her aching head this morning. No, this afternoon, she acknowledged as she saw in horror what time it was.

The doorbell was still ringing. Whoever it was was very determined. What if Oliver had changed his mind and come back after all? What if...?

Her fingers were trembling so much that she could hardly tie the belt of her robe. Quickly she hurried into the hallway, leaving her bedroom door open, and went to open the door, her heart beating so fast that she could hardly breathe.

Only it wasn't Oliver, it was Henry.

Henry!

Dumbly Lisa stood to one side as he walked self-importantly into her flat without bothering to close the door. Henry—what on earth was he doing here? What did he want? He was the last person Lisa wanted to see.

She pressed her fingers to her throbbing head. How could she have been stupid enough to think it might be Oliver? So much for all her promises to herself last night, as they'd all waited for midnight to come and the new year to start, that she would put him completely out of her mind and her heart.

'Henry, what is it? What are you doing here? What do you want?' she demanded shortly.

As she watched him breathe in then puff out his cheeks disapprovingly when he looked at her, she wondered how on earth she could ever have contemplated marrying him, how she had ever been so blind to the true reality of his character, his small-mindedness and fussiness, his lack of humour and generosity. Disapproval was written all over him as he looked at her.

'Surely you weren't still in bed?' he criticised her.

'No, I always dress like this. Of course I was still in bed,' Lisa snapped, losing her patience with him. She could hear him clearing his throat, the sound grating on her over-stretched nerves. If she had known it was only Henry at the door she would have stayed where she was.

'Mother thought I should come and see you,' he told her.

Lisa stared at him in angry disbelief.

'Your mother wanted you to come and see *me*... What on earth for? I would have thought I was the last person she would want you anywhere near. In fact, if I remember correctly, she said—'

'Er—yes, well...' Henry was flushing slightly as he cut her off. Why had she never noticed that slightly fishy bulge to his eyes when he was under pressure? Lisa wondered distastefully. Why had she never noticed, either, how very like his mother's his features were? She shuddered.

'The thing is, Lisa, that Mother thought I should make the situation absolutely clear to you, and—'

'What situation?' she demanded.

'Well...' Henry tugged at his collar. 'The thing is that I'm getting married to...to someone I've known for some time. She and I... Well, anyway, the wedding will be in June and we're having our official engagement party in February and...'

'And what?' Lisa pressed, irritated, wondering what on earth Henry's engagement and intended marriage had to do with her and why his mother should think she might want to hear about them.

He coughed and told her. 'Well, Mother didn't want there to be any misunderstandings...or embarrassment... She felt that it was best that you knew what was happening just in case you tried...'

Lisa couldn't believe what she was hearing.

'Just in case I tried what?' she demanded with ominous calm. 'Just in case I tried to resuscitate our relationship—is *that* what you're trying to say?' she asked him sharply. 'Is that what your mother is afraid of?'

Did either of them really think... after what had been said, after the accusations which had been made, that she wanted anything... *anything* to do with Henry? Heavens, she wouldn't so much as cross the street to say hello to him now, never mind try to resuscitate a relationship which Oliver had been quite right to tell her she was better off without, and she opened her mouth to tell Henry as much and then closed it again.

There was no point in losing her temper with Henry; rather, she ought to be pitying him.

'Who is the lucky bride-to-be?' she asked him with acid sweetness instead. 'Or can I guess...? Your aunt's god-daughter...?'

She saw from his expression that her guess had been right. Poor girl—Lisa hoped she knew what she was taking on.

'It's all right, Henry,' she reassured him calmly. 'I *do* understand and you are quite safe. In fact I wish you and your wife-to-be every happiness.'

And as she spoke she pulled open her front door and firmly pushed Henry backwards towards it whilst at the same time raising herself on her tiptoes to place her hands on his shoulders and deposit a dismissive and cold contemptuous kiss on his cheek—just as Oliver crossed the foyer outside her flat and to all intents and purposes saw her with her arms around Henry and kissing him.

There was a second's tense silence as Lisa saw Oliver over Henry's shoulder, his face set in a mask of furious anger, and then Henry was backing away from her and almost scurrying past Oliver as he headed for the stairs, whilst Oliver strode towards her, ignoring him.

'Oliver!' Lisa exclaimed weakly. 'What are *you* doing here? I wasn't expecting you. I thought you were in New York.'

'Very evidently,' Oliver agreed tautly as he slammed the front door behind him, enclosing them both in the suddenly far too small space of her hallway.

'It's just as well your fiancé has decided to leave. I want to have a few words with you... Not very brave of him, though. Some husband he's going to make... When I heard that your engagement was back on I couldn't believe it. I thought there must have been some mistake.'

'There has,' Lisa agreed. If only her head would stop aching, she thought.

'I tried to ring you from the airport,' she heard Oliver tell her.

'I was out at a party,' she responded.

'A party—to celebrate your engagement, no doubt,' he accused her grittily, adding savagely as he suddenly stiffened and looked past her and through her open bedroom door to where the clothes she had discarded the previous evening lay scattered all over the floor, 'Or did you save *that* until you were back here alone with him? My God, and to think I believed you when you told me that sexually he had never meant anything to you, that there had never been anything between you. What else did you lie to me about, Lisa? Not that it matters now...'

'I haven't lied to you,' Lisa protested, reminding him, 'And if anyone should be making any accusations surely it should be me? After all, I'm not the one who promised to be back for New Year's Eve and then broke that promise.'

Furious with herself, she closed her eyes. What on earth had prompted her to say that, to betray to him how much his broken promise had hurt her...how much *he* had hurt her?

'I had no choice,' she heard Oliver telling her angrily, 'but you did, Lisa, and you chose—'

'I chose nothing,' she interrupted him, as angry with him now as he patently was with her.

What right, after all, did he have to come back and make such ridiculous accusations—accusations he must surely know couldn't possibly be true? And how come he could manage to get back *now* when he hadn't been able to do so before?

'No?' Oliver strode past her and walked into her bedroom, demanding dangerously, 'No? Then would you mind explaining to me what the hell has been going on here?' He picked up the half-empty champagne glass that she had abandoned the previous evening and gestured to its now flat contents contemptuously as he snarled, 'Couldn't he even wait to let you finish this? *His* glass is empty I note...'

His glass?

Indignantly Lisa opened her mouth to put him right, but before she could say anything Oliver demanded savagely, 'It must have been quite some celebration the two of you had. What the hell did he do—tear the clothes off your back? You should have told me that that was what you liked,' he advised her, his voice suddenly dropping dangerously, his eyes glittering as his glance raked her from head to toe. 'I'd no idea your sexual tastes ran to such things. If I had—'

'Oliver, no...' she protested as he reached for her, catching hold of her arm and dragging her towards him as he ignored her angry denial.

'You don't understand,' she said, but he was beyond listening to reason or to any of her explanations, she realised, her heart lurching against her chest wall as she saw the way his gaze raked her, his look a mingling of loathing and desire.

'I think it's you who doesn't understand,' Oliver was correcting her softly, but there was nothing remotely soft about the way he was holding onto her or the way he was watching her. Her body trembled, her toes curling protestingly into the carpet. 'I thought we had something special, you and I... I thought I could believe in you, trust you... Like a fool I thought, when you told me you needed me, that you...

'What is it, what's wrong?' he asked her as he felt her body shiver and his apparent concern almost caught her off guard, until she saw the steely, almost cruel look in his eyes.

'Nothing's wrong,' Lisa denied. 'I just want you to let me go.'

'You're trembling,' Oliver pointed out, still in that same nerve-wrenchingly soft voice. 'And as for letting you go... I will let you go, Lisa, but not until I've reminded you of exactly why you shouldn't be marrying Henry...'

I'm not marrying Henry, Lisa wanted to say, but she only got as far as, 'I'm not—' before Oliver silenced her mouth, coming down hard on hers in a kiss of angry possession.

She tried to resist him and even physically to repel him, her own anger rising to meet his as she alternately tried to push him away and twist herself out of his grasp, but the more she fought to escape, the more her body came into contact with his, and as though something about her furious struggles only added extra fuel to the flames of his anger Oliver responded by propelling her back against the bedroom wall and holding her there with the hard strength of his body whilst he lifted her arms above her head and kept them pinioned there as he continued to brutalise her mouth with the savagery of his punishing kiss.

Lisa could feel his heart thudding heavily against her body, her own racing in frantic counterpoint, her breathing fast and uneven as her anger rose even higher. How dared he treat her like this? All thoughts of trying to explain and pacify him fled as she concentrated all her energy on trying to break free of him.

She could feel the heat coming off his body, the rough abrasion of the fabric of his clothes on her bare skin where her robe had come unfastened. Her mouth felt swollen and bruised from the savagery of his kisses, but there was no fear or panic in her; she recognised only an unfamiliar and fierce desire to match Oliver's fury with her own.

'You want me... Me...' she heard Oliver telling her thickly between plundering kisses.

'No,' she denied, but the sound was smothered by the soft moan that rose up in her throat as her body responded to its physical contact with his. Somehow, against all logic, against everything she herself had always thought she believed in, she was becoming aroused by him and by the furious force of their mutual anger, Lisa recognised. And so was he.

On a wave of shocked despair she closed her eyes, but that only made things worse; the feel of him, the scent of him, the weight of him against her—these were all so familiar to her aching, yearning body that they immediately fed her roaring, feral need, turning her furious attempt to wrench herself free from him into something that even to her came closer to a deliberately sensual indication of her body's need to be possessed by his than a genuine attempt to break free.

Her anger now wasn't just directed at him, it was directed at herself as well, but with it now she could feel a surge of sensual, languid weakness, a heat which seemed to spread irresistibly throughout her body, so that under the hard pressure of Oliver's searing kiss, instead of resisting him, her body turning cold and lifeless in rejection of him, she was actually moving, melting, yielding, moaning softly beneath her breath.

'Lisa, Lisa...' She could hear the responsive urgency in Oliver's voice, feel it in his hands as he released her pinioned arms to push aside her robe and caress her body.

Her anger was still there, Lisa saw as she watched him studying her semi-naked body, and so was his, but somehow it had been transmuted into a form of such intense physical desire that she could barely recognise either herself or him in the two human beings who had suddenly become possessed of such a rage of physical passion.

She had never dreamed that she could feel like this, want like this, react like this, she acknowledged dazedly several minutes later as she cried out beneath Oliver's savage suckling of her breast, clawing at his back in a response born not of anger or pain or fear but rather of a corresponding degree of intensity and compulsion.

And she made the shocking acknowledgement that there was something—some hitherto secret and sensually dark part of her—that actually found pleasure... that actually wanted savagery, a sensation that was only seconds away from actual pain, that a part of her needed this release of her pent-up emotions and desires, that this dark self-created floodtide of their mutual fury and arousal possessed a dangerously addictive alchemy that made her go back for more, made her cling dizzily to him as he wrenched off his clothes and lifted her, still semi-imprisoning her, against the wall.

He entered her with an urgency that could have been demeaning and unwanted and even painful but which was, in fact, so intensely craved and needed by her body that even she was caught off guard by the intensity of her almost instantaneous orgasm and by her inner knowledge that this was how she had wanted him, that part of her had needed that kind of appeasement, as Oliver allowed her to slide slowly down towards the floor.

Shocked, not just at what had happened but by Oliver's behaviour and even more so by her own, Lisa discovered that she was trembling so much that she had to lean against the wall for support. Ignoring the hand that Oliver put out to steady her, she turned away from him. She couldn't bear to look at him, to see the triumph and the contempt she knew would be in his eyes.

'Lisa...'

Whatever it was he was going to say she couldn't bear to listen to it.

'Just go,' she told him woodenly. 'Now... I never want to see you again... Never...'

She could hear her voice starting to rise, feel herself starting to tremble as shock set in. Her face burned scarlet with mortification as she reached for her abandoned robe and pulled it around her body to shield her nakedness as Oliver got dressed in grim-faced silence. Now that it was over she felt sick with disbelief and shock, unable to comprehend how she could have behaved in the way that she had, how she could have been so... so... depraved, how she could have wanted...

'Lisa...'

Oliver was dressed now and standing by the door. A part of her could sense that he too had behaved in a way that was out of character but she didn't want to listen to him. What was the point? He had shown her with damning clarity just what he thought of her.

'No... don't touch me...'

For the first time panic hit her as she saw him turn and start to walk towards her. She couldn't bear him to touch her now, not after...

She could sense him, feel him willing her to look at him but she refused to do so, keeping her face averted from him.

'So that's it, then,' she heard him saying hoarsely. 'It's over...'

'Yes,' she agreed. 'It's over.'

It wasn't until well over an hour after he had gone, after she had cleaned the bedroom from top to bottom, changed the bed, polished every piece of furniture, thrown every item of discarded clothing into the washing machine and worked herself into a furore that she realised that she had never actually told Oliver that she and Henry were not getting married. She gave a small, fatalistic shrug. What did it matter? What did *anything* matter any more after the way the pair of them had destroyed and abused their love?

Their *love* . . . There had never been any love—at least not on Oliver's side. Only lust; that was all.

Lisa shuddered. How had it happened? How could anger—not just his but, even worse, her own—become so quickly and so fatally transmuted into such an intensity of arousal and desire? Even now she could hardly believe it had happened, that *she* had behaved like that, that she had felt like that.

Later she would mourn the loss of her love; right now all she wanted to do was to forget that the last few hours had ever happened.

CHAPTER NINE

LISA woke up with a start, brought out of her deep, exhausted sleep, which she had fallen into just after the winter dawn had started to lighten the sky, by the shrill bleep of her alarm.

Tiredly she reached out to switch it off. She had spent most of the night lying in bed trying not to think about what had happened—and failing appallingly. Round and round her thoughts had gone until she'd been dizzy with the effort of trying to control them.

Shock, anger—against herself, against Oliver—grief, pain, despair and then anger again had followed in a relentless, going-nowhere circle, her final thought before she had eventually fallen asleep being that she must somehow stop dwelling on what was now past and get on with her life.

Her head ached and her throat felt sore—a sure sign, she suspected, that she was about to go down with a heavy cold. The faint ache in her muscles and her lethargy were due to another cause entirely, of course.

Quickly she averted her gaze from the space on the bedroom wall—the place where Oliver had held her as he...as they... The heat enveloping her body had nothing to do with her head cold, Lisa acknowledged grimly, and nor had the hot colour flooding her face.

It was bad enough that she had actually behaved in such an...an abandoned, yes, almost sexually aggressive way in the first place, but did her memory *have* to keep reminding her of what she had done, torturing her with it? she wondered wretchedly. She doubted that

Oliver was tormented by any such feelings of shame and guilt, but then, of course, it was different for a man. A man was allowed to be sexually driven, to express anger and hurt.

But it hadn't been Oliver's behaviour—hurtful though it had been—that had kept her awake most of the night, she acknowledged; it had been her own, and she knew that she would never be able to feel comfortable about what she had done, about the intensity of her passion, her lack of control, her sexuality, unchecked as it had been by the softening gentleness of love and modesty.

Women like her did not behave like that—they did *not* scratch and bite and moan like wild animals, they did *not* urge and demand and incite... they did *not* take pleasure in meeting... in matching a man's sexual anger, they did *not*... Lisa gave a low moan and scrambled out of bed.

There was no point in going over and over what had happened. It wouldn't change anything; *she* couldn't change anything. How on earth *could* Oliver have possibly thought that she could want *any* other man, never mind a sorry specimen like Henry...? How could he have misinterpreted... accused her...?

Angrily she stepped into the shower and switched it on.

That was the difference between men and women, she decided bitterly. Whereas she as a woman had given herself totally, emotionally, physically, mentally to Oliver, committing herself to him and to her love in the act of love—an act which she naïvely had believed had been a special and a wonderful form of bonding between them—to Oliver, as a man, they had simply had sex.

Sex. She started to shudder, remembering. Stop thinking about it, she warned herself grimly.

As she dried her hair and stared into the mirror at her heavy-eyed, pale-faced reflection she marvelled that such a short space of time could have brought so many changes to her life, set in motion events which had brought consequences that she would never be able to forget or escape.

Such a few short days, and yet they had changed her life for ever—changed *her* for ever. And the most ironic thing of all was that even if Henry or another man like him were to offer her marriage now she could not accept it. Thanks to Oliver she now knew that she could never be content with the kind of marriage and future which had seemed so perfect to her before.

Fergus her boss gave her an uneasy look as he heard her sneezing. He had a thing about germs and was a notorious hypochondriac.

'You don't sound very well,' he told Lisa accusingly as she started to open the mail which had accumulated over the Christmas break. 'You've probably caught this virus that's going round. There was something on last night's TV news about it. They're advising anyone who thinks they've got it to stay at home and keep warm...'

'Fergus, I've got a cold, that's all,' Lisa told him patiently. 'And besides, aren't we due to go down to Southampton on Thursday to start cataloguing the contents of Welton House?'

Welton House had been the property of one of Fergus's clients, and following her death her family had asked Fergus to catalogue its contents with a view to organising a sale. Normally it was the kind of job that Lisa loved, and she thought that it would do her good to get away from London.

'That's next week,' Fergus told her, his voice quickening with alarm as Lisa burst into another volley of sneezes. 'Look, my dear, you aren't well. I really think you should go home,' he said. 'In fact, I insist on it. I'll ring for a taxi for you...'

There was no point in continuing to protest, Lisa recognised wearily; Fergus had quite obviously got it into his head that she was dangerously infectious, and, if she was honest, she didn't feel very well. Nothing to do with her slight head cold, though. The pain that was exhausting her, draining every bit of her energy as she fought to keep it at bay had its source not in her head but in her emotions.

Her telephone was ringing as she unlocked her door; she stared at it for a few seconds, body stiffening. What if it was Oliver, ringing to apologise, to tell her that he had made a mistake, that he...?

Tensely she picked up the receiver, unsure of whether to be relieved or not when she heard her mother's voice on the other end of the line.

'Darling, I'm glad I caught you. I'm just ringing to wish you a Happy New Year. We tried to get through yesterday but we couldn't. How are you? Tell me all about your Christmas with Henry...'

Lisa couldn't help herself; to her own consternation and disbelief she burst into tears, managing to tell her mother between gulped sobs that she had not, after all, spent Christmas with Henry.

'What on earth has happened?' she heard her mother enquiring solicitously. 'I thought you and Henry—'

'It's not Henry,' Lisa gulped. 'He's getting married to someone else anyway. It's Oliver...'

'Oliver. Who's Oliver?' her mother asked anxiously, but the mere effort of saying Oliver's name had caused her so much pain that Lisa couldn't answer her questions.

'I've got to go, Mum,' Lisa fibbed, unable to bear any more. 'Thanks for ringing.'

'Lisa,' she could hear her mother protesting, but she was already replacing the receiver.

There was nothing she wanted to do more than fling herself on her bed and cry until there were no more tears left, until she had cried all her pain away, but what was the point of such emotional self-indulgence?

What she needed, she acknowledged firmly, was something to keep her thoughts away from Oliver not focused on him. It was a pity that the panacea that work would have provided had been taken away from her, she fretted as she stared round her sitting room, the small space no longer a warm, safe haven but a trap imprisoning her with her thoughts, her memories of Oliver.

Impulsively she pulled on her coat. She needed to get away, go somewhere, anywhere, just so long as it was somewhere that wasn't tainted with any memories of Oliver.

Oliver was in a foul mood. He had flown straight back to New York after his confrontation with Lisa, ostensibly to conclude the negotiations he had left hanging fire in his furious determination to find out what was going on. Well, he had found out all right. He doubted if he would ever forget that stomach-sickening, heart-destroying, split second of time when he had seen Lisa— *his* Lisa—in Henry's arms.

And as for what had happened . . . His mouth hardened firmly as he fought to suppress the memory of how easily—how very and humiliatingly easily—with Lisa in his arms he had been on the point of begging her to change her mind, of pleading with her at least to give him a chance to show her how good it could be for them.

He had known, of course, how reluctant, how wary she had been about committing herself fully to him, how afraid she had been of her own suppressed, deeply passionate nature. Then it had seemed a vulnerability in her which had only added to his love for her. Then he had not realised ... How could he have been so blind—he of all people? How could *she* have been so blind? Couldn't she see what they had had ... what they *could* have had?

The American negotiations were concluded now and he and Piers were on their way back north. They had flown back into London four hours ago to cold grey skies and thin rain.

'Oliver, is something wrong?'

He frowned, concentrating on the steely-grey ribbon of the motorway as he pulled out to overtake a large lorry.

'No, why should there be?' he denied, without looking at his cousin.

'No reason. Only you never explained why you had to fly back home like that and since you flew back to the States...well, it's obvious that something is bothering you. You're not having second thoughts about selling off part of the business, are you?' Piers asked him.

Oliver relaxed slightly, and without taking his eyes off the road responded, 'No, it was the right decision, but the timing could, perhaps, have been better. When is Emma due back?' he asked, changing the subject.

His cousin's girlfriend had been away visiting her family, and to his relief Piers, not realising that he was being deliberately sidetracked, started to talk enthusiastically about the reunion with her.

'It's official, by the way,' he informed Oliver. 'We're definitely going to get married this summer. In Harrowby if that's OK with you. We thought...well, I thought with Emma's family being so scattered... We...we're not sure how many of them will want to come up for the wedding yet, but the house is big enough to house twenty or so and...' He paused and gave Oliver a sidelong glance.

'I...I'd like you to be my best man, Oliver. Funny things, women,' he added ruminatively. 'Up until we actually started talking properly about it Emma had always insisted she didn't want a traditional wedding, that they were out of date and unnecessary, and yet now...she wants the whole works—bridesmaids, page-boys... She says it's to please her mother but I know different.

'That will mean two big weddings for Harrowby this summer. I still can't get over old Henry getting married— or rather his mother allowing him to... Hell, Oliver...watch out!' he protested sharply as his cousin suddenly had to brake quickly to avoid getting too close to the car in front.

'You're sure you're OK?' he asked in concern. 'Perhaps we should have stayed in London overnight instead of driving north straight from the flight. If you're tired, I can take over for a while...'

Oliver made no reply but his mouth had compressed into a hard line and there was a bleak, cold look in his eyes that reminded Piers very much of a younger Oliver just after he'd lost his mother. Something was bothering his cousin, but Piers knew him well enough to know that Oliver wasn't likely to tell him or anyone else exactly what it was.

'What the hell is that still doing here?'

Piers frowned as Oliver glared at the Christmas tree in the hallway. There was nothing about it so far as he could see to merit that tone of icy, almost bitter hatred in his cousin's voice. In fact, he decided judiciously, it was a rather nice tree—wilting now slightly, but still...

'It's not Twelfth Night until tomorrow,' he pointed out to Oliver. 'I'll give you a hand dismantling it then, if you like, and—'

'No,' Oliver told him curtly. 'I'll give Mrs Green a ring and ask her to arrange for Tom to come in and do it. We're going to be too busy catching up with everything that's been going on whilst we've been in New York.'

Thoughtfully Piers followed Oliver into the kitchen. It wasn't like his cousin to be so snappy and edgy, and, in point of fact, he had planned to drive across to York to see his parents whilst they were in the north, but now it seemed as though Oliver had other plans for him.

'Well, if we're going to work I'd better go and unpack and have a shower, freshen up a bit,' he told Oliver.

Upstairs he pushed open the door of the room which traditionally was his whenever he visited. The bed was neatly made up with crisp, clean bedlinen, the room spotless apart from...

Piers' eyes widened slightly as he saw the small, intimate item of women's clothing which Mrs Green had obviously laundered and left neatly folded on the bed, no doubt thinking that the small pair of white briefs belonged to Emma.

Only Piers was pretty sure that they didn't. So who did they belong to and where was their owner now?

Piers knew enough about his cousin to be quite sure that Oliver would not indulge in any kind of brief, meaningless sexual fling. Piers had endured enough lectures from his elder cousin on that subject himself to know that much.

So what exactly was going on? Oliver had made no mention to him of having any visitors recently, either male or female. He could always, of course, show him the briefs and ask him who they belonged to, but, judging from his current mood, such an enquiry was not likely to be very well received.

Another thought occurred to Piers. Was there any connection between the owner of the briefs and his cousin's present uncharacteristic bad mood?

When Piers returned downstairs Oliver was in his study opening the mail that had accumulated in his absence.

'Mmm...isn't it amazing how much junk gets sent through the post?' Piers commented as he started to help him. 'Oh, this one looks interesting, Oliver—an invite to Henry's betrothal party. Well, they certainly are doing things the traditional way, aren't they?'

'Give that to me,' Oliver instructed, his tone of voice so curt that Piers started to frown. He knew that Oliver had never particularly liked either Henry or his parents, especially his mother, but, so far as he knew, the anger he was exhibiting now was completely different from his normal attitude of relaxed indifference towards them.

Silently Piers handed him the invitation and saw the way Oliver's hands trembled slightly as he started to tear the invitation in two, and then he abruptly stopped, his concentration fixed on the black script which he had previously merely been glancing at furiously, his whole body so still and tense that Piers automatically moved round the desk to stand beside him, wondering what on earth it was that was written on the invitation that was causing such a reaction.

It had seemed unremarkable enough to him.

'"The betrothal is announced of Miss Louise Saunders, daughter of Colonel and Lady Anne Saunders, to—" Henry is marrying Louise Saunders,' Oliver intoned in a flat and totally unfamiliar voice.

'That's what it says,' Piers agreed, watching him in concern. 'It makes sense. They've known one another for ever and, of course, there's money in the family. Louise stands to inherit quite a considerable sum from her grandparents.

'Oliver, what is it, what's wrong?' he demanded as he saw the colour draining out of his cousin's face, leaving it grey and haggard, the skin stretched tightly over his facial bones as he lifted his head and stared unseeingly across the room.

'Nothing,' he told Piers tonelessly. 'Nothing.' And then he added in a sharper more incisive voice, 'Piers, there's something I have to do. I need to get back to London. I'll leave you here...'

'London...? You can't drive back there now,' Piers protested. 'It's too late. You haven't had any sleep in the last twenty-four hours that I know of, and not much in the three days before that. Oliver, what's going on? I—'

'Nothing's going on,' Oliver denied harshly.

'Look, if you must go back to London, at least wait until the morning when you've had some sleep,' said Piers. 'Surely whatever it is can wait that long?'

'Maybe it can,' Oliver agreed savagely, 'but *I* can't.'

In London Lisa's cold had turned into the full-blown virus, just as Fergus had predicted. Common sense told her that she ought to see a doctor but she felt too full of self-pity, too weak, too weighed down with misery to care how ill she was. And so instead she remained in her flat curled up in her bed, alternately sweating and shivering and being sick, wishing that she could just close her eyes and never have to open them again.

At first when she heard the sound of someone knocking urgently on her door after ten o'clock at night she thought she was imagining things, and then when the knocking continued and she realised that it was, in fact, real her heart started to bang so fiercely against her chest wall that it made her feel even more physically weak.

It was Oliver! It had to be. But it didn't matter what he had to say because she wasn't going to listen. She had always known that sooner or later he would discover his mistake. But nothing—no amount of apologising on his part—could take away the pain he had caused her.

If he had really loved her he would never have doubted her in the first place. *If* he had really loved her he would never...

The knocking had stopped, and Lisa discovered that she was almost running in her sudden urgency to open the door.

When she did so, flinging it wide, Oliver's name already on her lips, it wasn't Oliver who was standing there at all...

It was...

She blinked and then blinked again, and then to her own consternation she burst into tears and flung herself into the arms that had opened to hold her, weepingly demanding, 'Mother, what are you doing here?'

'You sounded so unhappy when I rang that I was worried about you,' her mother told her.

'You came all the way home from Japan because you were worried about me?'

Lisa stared at her mother in disbelief, remembering all the times when, as a child, she had refused to give in to her need to plead for her parents to return from whatever far-flung part of the world they were working in, telling herself stoically that she didn't mind that they weren't there, that she didn't mind that they didn't love her enough to be with her all the time.

'Don't sound so surprised,' her mother chided her gently. 'You may be an adult, Lisa, but to us, your father and me, you are still our child... Your father wanted to come with me, but unfortunately...' She spread her hands.

'Now,' she instructed as she smoothed Lisa's damp hair back from her forehead and studied her face with maternal intuition, 'tell me what's really wrong... All of it... Starting with this Oliver...'

'Oliver...'

Lisa shook her head, her mouth compressing against her emotions.

'I can't,' she whispered, and then added, 'Oh, Mum, I've been such a fool. I thought he loved me... I thought...'

'Oh, my poor darling girl. Come on, let me put the kettle on and make us both a drink and something to eat. You need it, by the looks of you. You're so thin... Oh, Lisa, what have you been doing to yourself?'

Half an hour later, having been bullied into having a hot bath by her mother, Lisa was ensconced on her small sofa, wrapped in her quilt, dutifully eating the deliciously creamy scrambled eggs that her mother had cooked for her whilst the latter sat on a chair opposite, waiting for her to finish eating before exclaiming as she removed the empty plate, 'Right, now! First things first—*who* is this Oliver?'

'He's... He's...' Lisa shook her head. 'I hate him,' she told her mother emotionally, 'and it hurts so much. He said he loved me but he couldn't have done—not and said what he did...'

Slowly, under her mother's patient and gentle questioning, the whole story came out. Although Lisa would not have said that she was particularly close to her parents, she had always felt able to talk to them. But, even so, she was slightly shocked to discover how easy it was to confide in her mother and how much she wanted to talk to her. Of course, there were bits she missed out—things so personal that she could not have discussed them with anyone. But she sensed from her mother's expression that she guessed when Lisa was withholding things from her and why.

Only when it came to outlining what had happened the night that Oliver had discovered her kissing Henry did her voice falter slightly.

'It must have been a shock for him to find Henry here,' her mother suggested when Lisa had fallen silent.

'He seemed to think that I was going to marry Henry. I...'

'And you told him, of course, that you weren't?' her mother offered.

Lisa shook her head. 'I tried to but...' She bit her lip, turning away, her face flushing slightly. 'He was so...

'I had been honest with him right from the start, told him why I was marrying Henry, told him that I hadn't... that I didn't think that sex...' She bit her lip again and stopped.

'After what had happened between us I don't understand how he could possibly have thought that I'd go back to Henry and to use what we had... all that we'd shared, to abuse it and destroy... To make me feel... How could he do that?' she whispered, more to herself than her mother.

'Perhaps because he's a man and because he felt jealous and insecure, because a part of him feared that what he had to offer you wasn't enough...that *he* wasn't enough.'

'But how could he possibly think that?' Lisa demanded, looking at her mother, her eyes dark and shadowed with pain. 'He knew how I felt about him, how I... He knew...'

'When you were in bed together, yes,' her mother agreed, softening the directness of her words with a small smile. 'But it isn't only our sex who fear that the emotions aroused when two people are sexually intimate may not be there once that intimacy is over.

'Your Oliver obviously knew he could arouse you, make you want him physically, but you had already told him that he was not what you wanted, what you had planned for. He already knew that a part of you feared the intensity of the emotions he had for you and aroused in you. You said yourself that he was anxious for you to make a commitment to him.'

'Initially, yes. But later... when I tried to tell him how I felt just before he left for New York, he didn't seem to want to listen.'

'Perhaps because he was afraid of what you might say,' her mother suggested gently, adding, 'He had no way of knowing you were going to tell him that you had changed your mind, that you were ready to make the commitment you had previously told him he must wait for. For all he knew, you might have wanted to say something very different—to tell him in fact that you had changed your mind and didn't want him at all.'

'But he couldn't possibly have thought that,' Lisa gasped, 'could he? It isn't important now anyway,' she said tiredly. 'I can never forgive him for—'

'Is it really *Oliver* you can't forgive, or yourself?' her mother interposed quietly, watching as Lisa stared at her and then frowned.

'You said that he was angry... that he made love to you,' she reminded Lisa. 'That he used your feelings to punish and humiliate you. But you never said that you didn't want him, or that he hurt or abused you. Anger against the person we love when he is our lover can result in some very passionate sex.

'For a woman, the first time she discovers that fact, it can be very traumatic and painful because it goes against everything that society has told us we should want from sexual intimacy. It can seem very frightening, very alien, very wrong to admit that we found pleasure in expressing our sexuality and desire in anger and, of course, that it was the only way we could express it...'

'He was so angry with me,' Lisa told her mother, not making any response to what she had said but mentally digesting it, acknowledging that her mother had a point, allowing herself for the first time since it had happened to see her own uninhibited and passionate response to Oliver as a natural expression of her own emotions.

'Oliver was probably as shocked and caught off guard by what happened as you were,' her mother told her wryly.

'You're not the only one something like this has happened to, you know,' she added comfortingly. 'I can still remember the first time your father and I had a major row... I was working on a piece for a gallery showing and I'd forgotten that your father was picking me up to take me out to dinner... He came storming into my work room demanding to know what was more important to me—my work or him... I had just finished working on the final piece for the exhibition. He picked it up and threw it against the wall.'

Lisa stared at her mother in shock.

'Dad did that? But he always seems so laid back...so...'

'Well, most of the time he is, but this particular incident was the culmination of a series of small misunderstandings. He didn't take second place to my work at all, of course, but...'

'Go on—what happened, after he had broken the piece?' Lisa demanded, intrigued.

'Well, I'm ashamed to say that I was so angry that I actually tried to hit him. He caught hold of me, we struggled for a while and then...'

As her mother flushed and laughed, Lisa guessed what the outcome of their fight had been.

'Afterwards your father stormed off and left me there on my own... I vowed I wasn't going to have anything more to do with him, but then—well, I started to miss him and to realise that what had happened hadn't been entirely his fault.'

'So what did you do?' Lisa asked.

Her mother laughed. 'Well, I made a small ceramic heart which I then deliberately broke in two and I sent him one half of it.'

'What did he do?' Lisa demanded breathlessly.

'Well, not what I had expected,' her mother admitted. 'When I sent him the heart I had been trying to tell him that my heart was broken. I kept the other half hoping he would come for it and that we could mend the break, but when several days went by and he didn't I began to think that he had changed his mind and that he didn't want me any more.

'I was in despair,' she told Lisa quietly. 'Exactly the same kind of despair you are facing now, but then, just when I had given up hope, your father turned up one night.'

'With the broken heart,' Lisa guessed.

'With the mended heart,' her mother told her, smiling. 'The reason he had delayed so long before coming to see me had been because he had been having a matching piece to the broken one I had sent him made, and where the two pieces were bonded together he had used a special bond to, as he put it, ''make the mended heart stronger than it had been before and unbreakable''.'

'I never dreamed Dad could be so romantic!' Lisa exclaimed.

'Oh, he can,' her mother told her. 'You should have seen him the night you were born. He had desperately wanted you to be a little girl. He was overjoyed when you were born—we both were—and he swore that no matter where our work might take us, as long as it was physically possible, we would take you with us...'

Lisa could feel fresh tears starting to sting her eyes. All these years and she had misunderstood the motivation behind her parents' constant uprooting of her, had never known how much she was actually loved.

As they looked at one another her mother reached out and took Lisa's hand, telling her firmly, 'When Oliver comes to see you—and he will—listen to what he has to say, Lisa—'

'When,' Lisa interrupted her. 'Don't you mean if...?'

'No, I mean when.'

'But how could he believe I could go behind his back and return to Henry?'

'He's a man and he's vulnerable, as I've already told you, and sometimes, when we feel vulnerable and afraid, we do things which are out of character. You said yourself that losing his mother when he did made him feel wary of loving someone in case he lost them too. Such emotions, even when they're only felt subconsciously, can have a very dramatic effect on our actions.'

'He won't come back,' Lisa protested dully. 'I told him I never wanted to see him again. We both agreed it was over.'

'Well, in that case, why don't you come back to Japan with me?' her mother suggested prosaically.

'I can't... My job... Fergus—'

'Fergus would give you some extended leave if you asked him,' her mother told her. 'He adores you, you know that...'

'Not when he thinks I'm full of germs,' Lisa told her ruefully. 'I'd like to come back with you,' she added hesitantly, 'but...'

'But not yet,' her mother finished for her, getting up to kiss her gently on the forehead and tell her, 'Well, I'm going to be here for a few days so you've got time to change your mind. But right now you're going to bed and I'm going to ring your father. I promised him I would. He'll be worrying himself to death wondering if you're all right. Now, bed...'

'Yes, Mum.' Lisa yawned obediently.

It felt so good to have her mother here with her, to know that she was cared for and loved, but no amount of parental love, no matter how valued, could erase the pain of losing Oliver.

He'll be back, her mother had promised her. But would he? Had they perhaps between them destroyed the tender, vulnerable plant of their love?

CHAPTER TEN

PIERS had been right to caution him against driving back to London tonight, Oliver admitted as his concentration wavered and he found himself having to blink away the grittiness of his aching eyes as he tried to focus on the road. With all that adrenalin and anxiety pumping through his veins it should have been impossible to start drifting off to sleep, but the compulsion to yawn and close his eyes kept on returning.

Up ahead of him he could see the lights of a motorway service station. Perhaps it would be wiser for him to stop, even if it was only for a hot, reviving cup of coffee. He knew there was no point in his trying to sleep; how could he when all he could think of was Lisa and the injustice he had done her?

The motorway services were closer than he had thought; he had started to pull into the lane taking him off the motorway, when the metal barrier at the edge of the road loomed up in front of him. The shrill squeal of brakes was followed by the harsh sound of metal against metal and his head jolted forward, pain exploding all around him.

'If it's that bad why don't you go out for a walk? It will be cheaper than wearing the carpet out.'

Lisa frowned as she looked at her mother.

'You've been pacing up and down the sitting room for the last half-hour,' her mother pointed out. 'And besides, it will do you good to get some fresh air.'

'Yes, perhaps you're right,' Lisa agreed. 'A walk might do me good.'

'Put your jacket on and some gloves,' her mother instructed her as Lisa headed for the hallway. 'I know the sun is out but we had frost last night.'

'Yes, Mother,' Lisa agreed dutifully, amusement briefly lightening her eyes and touching her mouth.

It had been three days since her mother's unexpected arrival now; in another two she would be returning to Japan. She was still pressing Lisa to return with her, and Lisa knew that she had spoken the truth when she had said that Fergus would give her the extra leave. There had been plenty of occasions in the past when she had put in extra hours at work, given up weekends and been cheerfully flexible about how long she worked. No, it wasn't the thought of Fergus that was stopping her.

'Why don't you come with me?' she suggested to her mother as she pulled on her jacket and found her gloves. The virus she had picked up had been thankfully short-lived, but Fergus had insisted that she did not return to work for at least a full week, and although she was enjoying her mother's company there were times when she was filled with restless energy that nothing seem to dissipate—a sense of urgency and anxiety.

Both of them knew what was causing it, of course, but since the night she had confided in her mother neither of them had ever referred to Oliver—Lisa because she couldn't bear to, couldn't trust herself to so much as think, never mind say his name, without losing control and being swamped by her emotions, and her mother, she suspected, because despite her initial conviction that Oliver would discover the truth and want to make amends she too was now beginning to share Lisa's belief that it was over between them.

'I won't be too long,' she told her mother as she opened the front door.

'No... there's an exhibition on at the Tate that I thought we might go to this afternoon, and then I thought we might have dinner at that Italian place in Covent Garden that your father likes so much.'

Her mother was doing her best to keep her occupied and busy, Lisa knew, and she was doing all she could to respond, but both of them also knew that she was losing weight and that she didn't sleep very well at night, and that sometimes when she did she woke up crying Oliver's name.

Her head down against the sharp January wind, she set off in the direction of the park.

Once she had gone Lisa's mother picked up the receiver and dialled her husband's number in Japan.

'I still haven't managed to persuade Lisa to come back with me,' she told him after they had exchanged hellos. 'I'm worried about her, David. She looks so pale and thin... I wish there was some way we could get in touch with this Oliver. No, I know we mustn't interfere,' she agreed, 'but if you could see her. She looks so... I must go,' she told him. 'There's someone at the door.' Quickly she replaced the receiver and went to open the front door.

The tall, dark-haired man wearing one arm in a sling with a huge, purpling bruise on his cheekbone and a black eye and a nasty-looking cut on his forehead was completely unfamiliar to her and yet she knew who he was immediately.

'You must be Oliver,' she told him simply, extending her hand to shake his. 'I'm so glad you're here. I'd just about begun to give up on you. Silly of me really, especially when... You look rather the worse for wear; have you been in an accident...? I'm Lisa's mother, by the way; she's out at the moment but she'll be back soon. Do come in...'

'I had a bump in my car a few days ago,' Oliver told her as he followed her into the flat. 'Fortunately nothing too serious. I say fortunately because it was my own fault; I virtually fell asleep at the wheel...' He caught the frowning look that Lisa's mother gave him and explained tersely, 'I was on my way back to London to see Lisa. Where did you say she was...?'

'She's gone out for a walk; she shouldn't be too long. She's been ill and I thought some fresh—'

'How ill?' Oliver pounced sharply.

Hiding her small, satisfied smile, Lisa's mother responded airily, 'Well, as a matter of fact, the doctor seemed quite concerned, but I'm a great believer in the efficacy of plenty of fresh air myself. She did say she felt a bit weak but—'

'A bit weak... Should she be out on her own?'

Poor man, he really had got it badly, Lisa's mother decided. As she witnessed his obvious concern Lisa's mother relented a little; this was no uncaring sexual predator, this was quite definitely a man very, very deeply in love.

'She's a lot better than she was,' she told him more gently.

Her half-hour in the park might have brought a pink flush to her skin and made her fingertips and toes tingle, Lisa acknowledged, but it had done nothing to alleviate the pain of loving Oliver. Only one person could do that, and with every day that passed her common sense told her that there was less and less chance of Oliver doing what her mother had claimed he was bound to do and coming in search of her, to tell her that he had discovered his mistake and to beg her to forgive him.

Grimly, Lisa retraced her steps towards her flat. Part of her wished desperately that she had never met Oliver, that she had never been exposed to the agony of loving him and then losing him, and yet another part of her clung passionately to the memory of their brief time together.

As her mother opened the door to her knock she told Lisa, 'I'm just going out. Oh, and by the way, you've got a visitor.'

'Oliver?'

Hope, disbelief, the desire to push open the door and run to him and the equally strong desire to turn on her heels and run from him were all there in Lisa's eyes.

'Treat him gently,' her mother advised her as she took hold of her and gave her a supportive hug.

'Treat him gently', after what he had done to her? In a daze Lisa walked past her mother and into the flat, closing the door behind her. Oliver was actually here...here. The angry relief that flooded her was that same emotion so familiar to parents when a child had emerged unscathed from a forbidden risk—relief at its safety and anger that it should have taken such a risk with itself, with something so precious and irreplaceable.

In fact she was so angry that she was actually shaking as she pushed open the sitting-room door, Lisa discovered, her mouth compressing, and without even waiting to look directly at Oliver, without daring to take the risk of allowing her hungry heart, her starved senses to feast on the reality of him, she demanded tersely, 'What are you doing here?'

He was standing with his back to her, facing the window, apparently absorbed in the view outside. He must have seen her walking back to the flat, Lisa recognised, her heart giving a small, shaky bound. He turned round and every single thought, every single word

she had been about to voice vanished as Lisa saw his cut
and bruised face, his arm in a sling.

'Oliver...' Her voice cracked suddenly, becoming
thready and weak, her eyes mirroring her shock and
anxiety as she whispered, 'What's happened? Why...?'

'It's nothing...just a minor bump in my car,' Oliver
assured her quickly. 'In fact I got off far more easily
than I deserved.'

'You've been in an accident. But how?' she demanded, ignoring his attempts to make light of his in-
juries and instinctively hurrying towards him, realising
only when it was too late and she was standing within
easy distance of the free arm he stretched forward to her
just how physically close to him she actually was.

Immediately she raised her hand in an automatic
gesture of rejection, but Oliver had already stepped
forward and the hand she had lifted in the body-language
sign that meant 'No, keep away from me' was somehow
resting against his shirt-covered chest with a very different meaning indeed.

'Oliver,' she protested weakly, but it wasn't any use;
it wasn't just her legs and her body that were trembling
now, her mouth was trembling as well, tears spilling over
from her eyes as she said his name, causing Oliver to
groan and reach for her, cradling her against his body
with his good arm as he said, 'Lisa, darling, please
don't...please don't cry. I can't bear to see you unhappy. I'll never forgive myself for what I've done—
never. My only excuse is that I was half-crazed with
jealousy over Henry.'

'Jealous?' Lisa questioned. 'You actually believed...? You were jealous of Henry?' She couldn't quite
keep the disbelief out of her voice.

'Yes,' Oliver admitted ruefully. 'It all seemed to slot
so neatly into place—your reluctance to commit yourself

to me, the news that Henry was marrying an old flame, the sight of the two of you together. I know I over-reacted. I was jealous, vulnerable,' he told her simply. 'You'd already made it plain that I wasn't the kind of man you wanted for a husband. I knew how reluctant you'd been to commit yourself to me, to our love.

'I knew, as well, how much I was rushing you, pres-surising you, using the intensity of what we both felt for one another to win you over. I suppose a part of me will always be the child who felt that in dying my mother deliberately abandoned me. Logically I know that isn't what happened, but there's always that small worm of fear there—fear of losing the one you love—and the more you love someone, the greater the fear is. And I love you more than I can possibly tell you. I'm not trying to look for excuses for myself, Lisa; there aren't really any. What I did was...' He paused and shook his head as she touched his hand gently with understanding for what he was trying to say. 'At the time it seemed logical that you should have changed your mind, decided you pre-ferred the safe life you had already mapped out for yourself.'

'Oh, Oliver.' Lisa shook her head.

'I was wrong, I know, and what I did was... unforgivable...'

The bleakness in his eyes and voice made Lisa want to reach out and hold him, but she restrained herself. She was already in his arms, and once she touched him...

'I...I didn't know that loving someone could be like that,' she told him in a husky voice. 'That anger could... That physically... I felt so ashamed after you had gone,' she admitted shakily.

'To have wanted you the way I did, to have responded to you, said the things I did, when I knew that you weren't touching me out of love. I felt so...' She shook her head, unable to find the words to express her own sense of horror at what, at the time, had seemed to her to be her own totally unacceptable and almost abnormal behaviour.

'Being angry with someone doesn't stop you loving them,' Oliver told her quietly. 'I was angry, bitter—furiously, destructively so; I can't deny that. I wanted to hurt you in the same way that I felt you had hurt me, but those feelings, strong as they were, destructive as they were, did not stop me loving you. In fact...'

He paused and looked down into her upturned face, searching her eyes before telling her roughly, 'I tried to tell myself that I was punishing you... that I *wanted* to punish you... but almost from the moment I held you in my arms...' He stopped and shook his head. 'No matter what I might have *said*, my *body* was loving you, Lisa—loving you and wanting you and hating me for what I was trying to do.'

'What made you think I was marrying Henry in the first place?' Lisa questioned him.

'My cousin,' he informed her briefly. 'Emma had phoned from Yorkshire and she'd heard that Henry was getting married to someone he had already known for some time.'

'And you assumed it was me...'

'I assumed it was you,' Oliver agreed.

A little uncertainly Lisa looked up at him. The sadness she could see in his eyes made her heart jolt against her ribs.

'Have I completely ruined everything between us?' he asked her huskily. 'Tell me I haven't Lisa. I can't... Being without you these last few days has been hell, but if you...'

He paused and Lisa told him shakily, 'I've missed you as well...'

Missed him!

'I should have rung you from New York and talked to you instead of flying back like that, but it looked like those damned negotiations were going to go on for ever and I'd already missed being with you on New Year's Eve. And then when I reached your flat and saw you there with Henry...'

'He came to tell me that he was getting married. His mother had sent him,' Lisa explained drily. 'She was concerned that I might get in touch with him and try to patch up our differences... I had just finished telling Henry that there was absolutely no chance whatsoever of that happening when you appeared. I thought when you didn't make New Year's Eve that you were having second thoughts...about us,' she confessed.

'*Me* having second thoughts... There's no way I could ever have second thoughts about the way I feel about you...about what I want with you...'

Lisa took a deep breath. There was something she had to tell him now, whilst they were both being so open and honest with one another.

'I did,' she confessed. '*I* had second thoughts...the day we parted...' She looked anxiously up at him; his face was unreadable, grave, craven almost, as he watched her in silence.

'I tried to tell you then,' she hurried on. 'I tried to say that I had changed my mind, but you didn't seem to want to listen and I thought that perhaps you had changed yours and that—'

'Changed your mind about what?' Oliver demanded hoarsely, cutting across her.

'About...about wanting to make a commitment,' Lisa admitted, stammering slightly as she searched his face anxiously, looking for some indication as to how he felt about what she was saying, but she could see none. Her heart started to hammer nervously against her ribs. Had she said too much? Had she...? Determinedly she pushed her uncertainty away.

'I knew then that it was just fear that had stopped me from telling you what I already knew... That I *did* love you and that I did want to be with you... I was even going to suggest that I went to New York with you.' She paused, laughing shakily. 'When it came to it I just couldn't bear the thought of not being with you, but you seemed so preoccupied and distant that I thought—'

'You were going to tell me that...?' Oliver interrupted her. 'Oh, my God, Lisa... Lisa...'

Any response she might have made was muffled by the hard pressure of his mouth against hers as, ignoring her protests that he might hurt his injured arm, he gathered her up, held her against his body and kissed her with all the hungry passion she had dreamed of in the time they had been apart.

'Lisa, Lisa, *why* didn't you say something to me?' Oliver groaned when he had finally finished kissing her. 'Why...?'

'Because I didn't think you wanted to hear,' Lisa told him simply. 'You were so distant and—'

'I was trying to stop myself from pleading with you to change your mind and come with me,' Oliver told her grimly. '*That* was why I was quiet.'

'Oh, Oliver...'

'Oh, Lisa,' he mimicked. 'How long do you suppose your mother will be gone?' he asked her as he bent his head to kiss her a second time.

'I don't know, but she did say something about going to see an exhibition at the Tate,' Lisa mumbled through his kiss.

'Mmm...' He was looking, Lisa noticed, towards the half-open bedroom door, and her own body started to react to the message she could read in his eyes as she followed his gaze.

'We can't,' she protested without conviction. 'What about your arm? And you still haven't told me about the accident,' she reminded him.

'I will,' he promised her, and added wickedly, 'They said at the hospital that I should get plenty of rest and that I shouldn't stand up for too long. They said that the best cure for me would be...' And he bent his head and whispered in Lisa's ear exactly what he had in mind for the two of them for the rest of the afternoon.

'Tell me about the accident first,' Lisa insisted, blushing a little as she saw the look he gave her when he caught that betraying 'first'.

'Very well,' he agreed, adding ruefully, 'Although, it doesn't make very good hearing.

'I didn't find out until we were back in Yorkshire that you weren't marrying Henry, but once I did and I realised what I'd done I broke all the rules and drove straight back here despite the fact that I hadn't had any sleep for going on three days and that I was jet-lagged into the bargain. Hardly a sensible or safety-conscious decision but...' He gave a small, self-deprecatory grimace. 'I was hardly feeling either sensible or safety-conscious; after all, what else had I got left to lose? I'd already destroyed the most precious thing I had in my life.

'Anyway... I must have started to doze off at the wheel; fortunately I'd already decided to stop at a motorway service station and I'd slowed down and pulled onto the approach road, and even more fortunately there was no other vehicle, no other person around to be involved in my self-imposed accident. The authorities told me that I was lucky my car was fitted with so many safety features... otherwise...'

'No, don't,' Lisa begged him, shuddering as her imagination painted an all too vivid picture of just how differently things could have turned out.

'Lisa, I know there is nothing I can say or do that can take away the memory of what I did; all I can do is promise you that it will never happen again and ask if you can forgive me.'

'It did hurt that you could think such a thing of me,' Lisa admitted quietly, 'and that you could... could treat me in such a way, but I *do* understand. In a way both of us were responsible for what happened; both of us should have trusted the other and our love more. If we had had more mutual trust, more mutual faith in our love then... Oh, Oliver,' she finished, torn between laughter and tears as she clung onto him. 'How could you possibly think I could even contemplate the idea of marrying anyone else, never mind Henry, after you... after the way you and I...?'

'Even when mentally I was trying to hate you I was still loving you physically and emotionally,' Oliver told her huskily. 'The moment I touched you... I never intended things to go so far; I'd just meant to kiss you one last time, that was all, but once I had...'

'Once you had what?' Lisa encouraged him, raising herself up on tiptoe to feather her lips teasingly against his.

'Once I had... this,' Oliver responded, smothering a groan deep in his throat as he pulled her against him with his good arm and held her there, letting her feel the immediate and passionate response of his body to her as he kissed her.

'We really ought to get up,' Lisa murmured sleepily, her words belying her actions as she snuggled closer to Oliver's side. 'The day's almost gone and...'

'Soon it will be bedtime. I know,' Oliver finished mock-wickedly for her. 'It was very thoughtful of your mother to telephone and say that she'd decided to go and visit some friends this evening and to stay overnight with them...'

'Mmm...very,' Lisa agreed, sighing leisurely as Oliver's hand cupped her breast.

'Mmm...that feels nice,' she told him.

'It certainly does,' Oliver agreed, and asked her softly, 'And does this?' as he bent his head and started to kiss the soft curve of her throat.

'I'm not sure... Perhaps if you did it for a bit longer,' Lisa suggested helpfully. 'A lot longer,' she amended more huskily as his mouth started to drift with delicious intent towards her breast... 'A lot, *lot* longer.'

EPILOGUE

'How does that look?'

Lisa put her head to one side judiciously as she studied the huge Christmas tree that Oliver had just finished erecting in the hallway.

'I think it needs moving a little to the left; it's leaning slightly,' she told him, and then laughed as she saw his pained expression.

'No, darling, it's perfect,' she added with a happy sigh. They had been married for eight months, their wedding having preceded both Henry's and Piers'. Lisa's parents had both flown home for the wedding and Lisa and Oliver had flown out to Japan to spend three weeks with them in October.

Fergus had been disappointed when Lisa had handed in her notice but she and Oliver were talking about the possibility of her setting up her own business in the north in partnership with Fergus. It seemed almost impossible to Lisa that it was almost twelve months since that fateful night when Oliver had found her stranded on the road and brought her home with him. Her smile deepened as she glanced down at the Armani suit she was wearing— a surprise gift from Oliver to mark the anniversary of the day they had initially met.

'Happy?' Oliver asked her, bending his head to kiss her.

'Mmm ... how could I not be?' Lisa answered, snuggling closer to him. 'Oh, Oliver, last Christmas was wonderful, special, something I'll never forget, but this Christmas is going to be special too; I'm so glad that everyone's been able to come—your family and my parents.'

'We're certainly going to have a houseful,' Oliver agreed, laughing.

He had raised his eyebrows slightly at first when Lisa had suggested to him that they invite all his own relatives and her parents to spend their Christmas with them, but Lisa's enthusiasm for the idea had soon won him over.

'You really do love all this, don't you?' he commented now, indicating the large hallway festooned now for Christmas with the garlands and decorations that Lisa had spent hours making.

'Yes, I do,' Lisa agreed, 'but not anything like as much as I love you. Oh, Oliver,' she told him, her voice suddenly husky with emotion, 'you've made me so happy. It's hard to imagine that twelve months ago we barely knew one another and that—I love you so much.'

'Not half as much as I love you,' Oliver whispered back, his mouth feathering against hers and then hardening as he felt her happy response.

'We still haven't put the star on the tree,' Lisa reminded Oliver through their kiss.

'*You* are my star,' he told her tenderly, 'and without you I'd be lost in the darkness of unhappiness. You light up my life, Lisa, and I never, ever want to be without you.'

'You never, ever will,' Lisa promised him.

'Hey, come on, you two, break it up,' Piers demanded, coming into the hallway carrying a basket of logs for the fire. 'You're married now—remember?'

'Yes, we're married,' Oliver agreed, giving Lisa a look that made her laugh and blush slightly at the same time, as he picked up the star waiting to be placed at the top of the tree—the final touch to a Christmas that would be all the things that Christmas should be, that Christmas and every day *would* be for her from now on.

Oliver *was* her Christmas, all her special times, her life, her love.

If you are looking for more titles by
PENNY JORDAN
Don't miss these fabulous stories by one of
Harlequin's most renowned authors:

Harlequin Presents®

#11552	SECOND-BEST HUSBAND	$2.89 ☐
#11599	STRANGER FROM THE PAST	$2.99 ☐
#11705	LAW OF ATTRACTION	$2.99 U.S. ☐
		$3.50 CAN. ☐
#11734	TUG OF LOVE	$3.25 U.S. ☐
		$3.75 CAN. ☐
#11746	PASSIONATE POSSESSION	$3.25 U.S. ☐
		$3.75 CAN. ☐
#11756	PAST LOVING	$3.25 U.S. ☐
		$3.75 CAN. ☐
#11774	YESTERDAY'S ECHOES	$3.25 U.S. ☐
		$3.75 CAN. ☐

Harlequin® Promotional Titles

#97120	SILVER	$5.95 ☐
#97121	THE HIDDEN YEARS	$5.99 ☐
#97122	LINGERING SHADOWS	$5.99 ☐

(limited quantities available on certain titles)

TOTAL AMOUNT	$
POSTAGE & HANDLING	$
($1.00 for one book, 50¢ for each additional)	
APPLICABLE TAXES*	$_____
TOTAL PAYABLE	$_____
(check or money order—please do not send cash)	

To order, complete this form and send it, along with a check or money order for the total above, payable to Harlequin Books, to: **In the U.S.:** 3010 Walden Avenue, P.O. Box 9047, Buffalo, NY 14269-9047; **In Canada:** P.O. Box 613, Fort Erie, Ontario, L2A 5X3.

Name: _____

Address: _____ City: _____

State/Prov.: _____ Zip/Postal Code: _____

*New York residents remit applicable sales taxes.
Canadian residents remit applicable GST and provincial taxes.   HPJBACK6

♦HARLEQUIN®

Look us up on-line at: http://www.romance.net

1997
Reader's Engagement Book
A calendar of important dates
and anniversaries for readers to use!

Informative and entertaining—with notable
dates and trivia highlighted throughout the year.

Handy, convenient, pocketbook size to help you
keep track of your own personal important dates.

Added bonus—contains $5.00 worth of coupons
for upcoming Harlequin and Silhouette books.
This calendar more than pays for itself!

Available beginning in November at
your favorite retail outlet.

HARLEQUIN ® Silhouette®

CAL97

Men who find their way to fatherhood—by
fair means, by foul, or even by default!

#1860 *A PROPER WIFE*
by
Sandra Marton

Ryan Kincaid and Devon Franklin aren't looking
to get married—especially not to each other! But
their families are making sure that the pressure
is on—and so is the wedding!

Available wherever
Harlequin books are sold.